# PROLOGUE: THE WEIGHT OF THE PRESENT

Calvin Mercer had once thought his life would amount to something greater. As he walked out of the military processing center for the last time, duffel bag slung over his shoulder, he had imagined the opportunities waiting for him. The discipline, the training, the technical skills he'd picked up—surely they would open doors. The world outside, however, didn't seem to care about what he had done or what he could do. Employers saw only another veteran with no combat experience, no prestigious degrees, just a guy who could troubleshoot circuits and fix hardware. A dime a dozen.

Now, five years later, he spent his days at a small Boston-based computer repair shop, swapping out motherboards, diagnosing software issues, and trying not to let the monotony grind him down. The customers were fine, his coworkers were fine, his paycheck was fine. It was all just... fine. He hadn't expected to become some celebrated war hero, but he had hoped for more than this. More than answering phones, replacing hard drives, and taking orders from managers who didn't know half as much about computers as he did.

The only escape from the drudgery was history.

Boston had always been a city drenched in its past, and Calvin immersed himself in it. After work, he often walked the Freedom Trail, running his fingers along the old bricks of buildings that had witnessed revolutions. He lingered in front of Faneuil Hall, imagining the heated debates of the Sons of Liberty echoing off the wooden beams. He stood at the site of the Boston Massacre, envisioning the riotous crowd, the crack of musket fire, the moment history pivoted.

On the bad days, he'd retreat to his small apartment, a place barely big enough for his bookshelves, let alone his ambitions. He'd lose himself in the pages of biographies and war journals, tracing the lives of men who had shaped the world. John Adams, Nathaniel Greene, Washington himself—men who had stood at the edge of the unknown and pushed forward, who had risked everything for something greater than themselves.

It gnawed at him, this feeling that he had somehow missed his purpose, that history had no place for someone like him. He was meant for more. He just didn't know how or why.

But soon, history would find him.

# THE PATRIOT PARADOX

# PART ONE

*The Ordinary Before the Impossible*

# CHAPTER 1: THE WEIGHT OF THE ORDINARY

Calvin's alarm buzzed at exactly 6:30 a.m., the same as it had every weekday for the past five years. He groaned, slapped the snooze button, and allowed himself another ten minutes before rolling out of bed. His apartment was small, cluttered with books and old computer parts—half projects he had started and never finished. He tossed on a wrinkled polo with the shop's logo embroidered over the chest and grabbed a stale granola bar from the kitchen counter before heading out the door.

At **Patriot Tech Repair**, the morning rush was the same as always. The first customer of the day was an elderly man clutching a laptop like it was a fragile relic.

"Stopped turning on," the man grumbled, sliding it across the counter.

Calvin flipped it over, popped the battery out, and held back a sigh. "This is at least ten years old. Might be time for a new one."

"Nonsense! I just need it to check emails and play Solitaire."

Calvin nodded, already diagnosing the issue in his head. "Give me an hour. I'll see what I can do."

As the man shuffled away, his coworker, Brandon, leaned against the counter. "Dude, you need to stop crushing dreams. Let the man live his Solitaire fantasy."

Calvin smirked. "You try explaining to a seventy-year-old why their hard drive is basically a ticking time bomb."

Brandon chuckled. "I'd rather not. That's your job."

At lunch, they grabbed sandwiches from the café next door and sat at a small table outside. Calvin stared out at the historic buildings lining the street, his fingers tapping absently on the table.

"You know," he said between bites, "the Boston Massacre happened just down the street. Five people killed. Started as a riot over British soldiers taking jobs from locals."

Brandon rolled his eyes. "Here we go again."

Calvin ignored him. "And the Tea Party? That happened right near the harbor. Bunch of pissed-off colonists threw an entire shipment of British tea overboard. Full-on rebellion in the making."

"You ever just eat a sandwich without giving a history lecture?" Brandon asked.

"Come on, man. We live in a city where history is literally around every corner. Paul Revere's house? Still there. The Old North Church? Still standing. This place is alive with the past."

Brandon sighed. "And yet here we are, fixing laptops."

Calvin leaned back in his chair, eyes still on the old buildings. "Yeah," he muttered. "Here we are."

The hours crawled by, filled with the same repetitive tasks—cracked screens, malware-riddled laptops, customers who swore they hadn't downloaded anything suspicious despite their desktops being littered with pop-ups. By the afternoon, Calvin had settled into the rhythm, resigned to another forgettable day.

Then the agents walked in.

They weren't customers. That much was obvious. Two men in dark suits, crisp and expressionless, stepped into the shop, scanning the room before their eyes locked onto Calvin. The taller of the two reached into his coat, and for the briefest moment, Calvin's pulse jumped—military reflex kicking in. But instead of a weapon, the man produced a badge.

"Mr. Mercer," the agent said, voice even and firm. "We need you to come with us."

Brandon whistled lowly. "Damn, Calvin. What'd you do?"

Calvin stared at the badge, then at the agents. "Uh… let's see some ID."

The taller agent smoothly reached into his jacket and produced a badge, followed by a picture ID. The stockier agent did the same. The credentials bore the emblem of an agency Calvin had never heard of before.

"What the hell is this? I've never heard of this department."

"You wouldn't have," the taller agent replied. "But it's legitimate."

Calvin studied the IDs, his gut telling him this was either a deep-cover government operation or the most elaborate scam he'd ever seen. His eyes skimmed over the embossed text at the top. **Division of Advanced Research Methods.**

"DARM?" Calvin said, squinting. "What, you guys out here doing top-secret government farming? Or is this where all the nerds go when DARPA won't take them?"

The shorter agent smirked but didn't respond.

Calvin let out a sharp breath. "So, are you actually going to tell me what this is about?"

The taller agent tucked his ID away. "You'll learn more once we arrive."

Calvin glanced at Brandon, who shrugged. The shop was dead for the afternoon, and it wasn't like he had anything better to do. With a resigned sigh, he grabbed his jacket.

"Fine," he muttered. "But if this is about my taxes, I swear—"

"Just come with us, Mr. Mercer," the taller agent said, already turning toward the door.

As Calvin followed them out, an uneasy feeling settled in his gut. Something about this wasn't normal. And for the first time in years, his life was about to become anything but ordinary.

# CHAPTER 2: THE RIDE TO THE UNKNOWN

Calvin sat stiffly in the back seat of the black SUV, his arms crossed tightly over his chest as the cityscape blurred past the tinted windows. The air in the vehicle felt heavier than it should, thick with an unspoken tension. The agents, silent and unyielding, sat in the front, their faces unreadable. Holt, the taller of the two, drove with an unwavering focus, while Grayson, the stockier one, occasionally glanced down at a folder resting on his lap, flipping through pages without ever looking back at Calvin.

"So," Calvin said, breaking the silence, his voice coming out more casual than he felt. "Where exactly are we going?"

Neither man responded immediately. Holt didn't even glance in the rearview mirror. Grayson, after a moment of hesitation, finally replied, "You'll be briefed when we arrive."

Calvin scoffed. "Right. Because that's not ominous at all."

A few beats of silence stretched between them, and Calvin felt the knot in his stomach tighten. He hated not knowing. He hated being in situations where he wasn't in control. The best thing he could do was keep talking, keep the atmosphere from feeling like he was on his way to an execution.

"You know," he started, eyeing the passing streets, "we just went by the site of the Great Molasses Flood of 1919. A storage tank burst and sent a fifteen-foot wave of molasses through the North End. Killed twenty-one people. Can you imagine? Drowning in syrup?"

Neither agent reacted.

Calvin huffed. "Tough crowd."

They drove in silence for a few more minutes before Calvin tried again. "Oh, and there—right past the bridge? That's where Dr. Joseph Warren was buried after Bunker Hill. Well, temporarily, anyway. The British tossed him into a mass grave, but his family eventually dug him up. You know how they identified him?" He paused, waiting for some kind of reaction. "A false tooth. Paul Revere made it for him. First recorded instance of dental forensics."

Grayson shifted slightly, exhaling through his nose. Not quite a laugh, but close. Holt remained as unshaken as a stone.

Calvin leaned back, letting out a slow breath. His hands were damp, and his pulse still had a little too much rhythm for his liking. He didn't like this—this feeling of being boxed in, of not knowing where he was going or why. But he wasn't about to let these guys see that.

Eventually, the city fell away, replaced by long stretches of empty highway. The SUV turned onto a road flanked by trees, and the deeper they went, the fewer signs of civilization there were. Finally, after passing through several gated checkpoints, they pulled up to a sprawling compound of nondescript gray buildings surrounded by high fences and security cameras. Armed guards patrolled the perimeter, their faces unreadable behind dark sunglasses.

Calvin swallowed hard. "This is the part where I start regretting getting in the car, isn't it?"

Holt finally turned around, his expression impassive. "Before we go inside, you'll need to sign a non-disclosure agreement."

Calvin raised an eyebrow. "You dragged me out here without telling me why, and now I have to sign an NDA?"

Grayson handed him a clipboard with a thick document attached. Calvin took it hesitantly, flipping through the pages. The text was dense, filled with legal jargon that made his eyes blur. He read a few sections aloud, his voice dripping with skepticism.

"'By signing below, the undersigned acknowledges potential exposure to classified research, experimental methodologies, and proprietary technologies, thereby waiving legal recourse in the event of physical, psychological, or—'" He stopped mid-sentence, blinking. "Wait. Temporal distress?"

Grayson didn't react. "Legal formality."

"Yeah, well, 'unanticipated anomalies' sounds like a pretty big umbrella. Should I be worried about spontaneous combustion?"

Holt sighed, clearly tired of the back-and-forth. "You're not a lawyer, Mercer. Neither are we. But if you want to know what's behind those doors, you need to sign."

Calvin glanced between them, then back at the document. Every rational part of him screamed that this was a bad idea. But the other part—the part that longed for something bigger than dead hard drives and tech support—kept him from tossing the clipboard back at them.

With a slow exhale, he grabbed the pen and scrawled his signature at the bottom.

Grayson took the clipboard back, glanced at it, then nodded. "Welcome aboard."

Holt opened the door, gesturing for Calvin to step out. As he did, the weight of the situation fully sank in. Whatever this was, there was no turning back now.

As they walked toward the main building, Calvin kept his hands in his pockets, glancing at the walls, the cameras, the guards.

The whole place screamed secrecy, like something out of a bad spy movie.

Just what the hell had he signed himself up for?

Inside, the facility had the sterile feel of a military installation. Fluorescent lights buzzed overhead, and the air smelled faintly of metal and antiseptic. Calvin's shoes echoed on the tile as they led him through a series of corridors, passing doorways marked with cryptic alphanumeric codes.

They entered a conference room, where a man in a crisp suit stood waiting.

"Mr. Mercer," the man greeted. "I'm Director Ellison. Welcome to the Division of Advanced Research Methods."

Calvin glanced at Holt and Grayson, who now stood at the back of the room. Their job was done—for now. Their postures had shifted subtly, less involved, more watchful. *So, they're my babysitters now.*

Ellison gestured to a chair. "Please, sit. We have much to discuss."

# CHAPTER 3: TERMS AND CONDITIONS

The conference room was sterile, windowless, and had the faint, clinical smell of recently cleaned surfaces. The walls were a dull, institutional gray, the kind of color that discouraged creativity, conversation, or any sense of comfort. A long steel table stretched down the middle of the room, its surface so polished that the overhead fluorescent lights created a sharp reflection. It felt more like an interrogation room than a place where job offers were made.

Calvin sat on one side, still gripping the armrests of his chair as though he were expecting turbulence. Across from him sat Director Ellison, a man in his late fifties with neatly combed silver hair and a suit that was so perfectly pressed it seemed unnatural. His presence radiated quiet authority, the kind that came from years of being in charge of things people weren't allowed to know about.

Behind Calvin, Holt and Grayson stood by the door like silent sentinels. Their job wasn't done yet.

Ellison clasped his hands together on the table and gave Calvin a measured look. "Mr. Mercer, let's start with the basics. You've been selected for a unique opportunity. This project is highly classified, and full disclosure will come in stages. For now, you only need to understand that your skills make you an excellent candidate for what we do here."

Calvin let out a sharp breath. "Yeah, see, that's the part I don't get. I fix computers. I'm not exactly CIA material."

Ellison smiled slightly, as if he'd expected the response. "Your technical background is only part of it. You also have military training, adaptability, and a strong problem-solving skillset. That combination is rare. You have the right kind of mind for this work."

Calvin narrowed his eyes. "What *is* this work?"

"For now, classified research and development," Ellison said smoothly. "Think of it as a highly specialized engineering role."

Calvin's skepticism deepened. "So, what, I'll be in some lab, working on top-secret government gadgets? Because, honestly, I don't see why you needed to drag me out here for that."

Ellison leaned forward slightly. "We're pushing the boundaries of what is currently possible. You'll be working alongside some of the brightest minds in the world. It's not just about fixing things, Mr. Mercer. It's about discovery."

Calvin studied him for a moment, trying to read between the lines. He'd heard enough corporate pitches to recognize when someone was deliberately leaving out the important parts.

"Alright," Calvin said finally. "So, do I have to quit my job?"

"No," Ellison replied. "For now, you will maintain your normal life. You will continue living at home. Your work schedule will be adjusted, but it will not interfere with your day-to-day responsibilities. Think of this as an extended contract. The only difference is, what you learn here stays here."

Calvin leaned back in his chair, crossing his arms. "And how much does this 'extended contract' pay?"

Ellison slid a folder across the table. Calvin opened it and his eyebrows shot up. It was more money than he had ever made—a *lot* more.

"Well, damn," Calvin muttered. "I'd ask what the catch is, but I'm pretty sure I already signed away my soul."

Ellison chuckled. "Not your soul, Mr. Mercer. Just your discretion."

Calvin flipped through the pages, skimming sections. Then something caught his eye.

"Hang on," he said, tapping a section with his finger. "'In the event of termination of employment, the undersigned agrees to submit to debriefing procedures to ensure information containment.'" He glanced up. "That sounds a lot like 'we'll make you disappear if you quit.'"

Ellison remained calm. "It simply means you will undergo exit procedures to ensure no classified information is compromised."

Calvin gave him a long, skeptical look. "Uh-huh. And 'exit procedures' doesn't sound ominous to you?"

"You have my assurance that they are standard security measures," Ellison said smoothly.

Calvin exhaled. "Alright, let's say I go along with this. What if I decide it's not for me?"

Ellison's smile never wavered. "You'll be released from your contract, and your access will be revoked. You will, however, still be bound by the non-disclosure agreement. Sharing anything about what you see or do here would be a violation of federal law."

Calvin glanced toward Holt and Grayson. Their expressions remained unreadable, but something about their presence told him that "released from the contract" might have broader implications than Ellison was letting on.

"Right," Calvin said. "And how do you plan to make sure I keep my mouth shut?"

Ellison's smile didn't waver. "That's what Agents Holt and Grayson are for."

Calvin sighed. "Great. So I get two new best friends shadowing me everywhere?"

Grayson smirked. "Don't worry, Mercer. We won't be sitting outside your apartment window with binoculars. Just routine check-ins."

Holt, however, remained stoic. "Just don't do anything stupid."

Calvin rubbed his temples. This was insane. But that number on the contract… that kind of money meant never worrying about bills, never struggling to get by. And despite his gut screaming at him, something inside him was intrigued. What the hell *was* this project?

"Alright," Calvin finally said, closing the folder. "I'm in."

Ellison nodded. "Excellent. Report back here tomorrow at 0800. Welcome to the team, Mr. Mercer."

Calvin stood, tucking the folder under his arm. As Holt and Grayson escorted him out of the room, he couldn't shake the feeling that he had just made a deal with the devil.

And he still had no idea what for.

# CHAPTER 4: A SLEEPLESS NIGHT

The ride home was quieter than the ride to the facility. Holt drove while Grayson sat in the passenger seat, flipping idly through some paperwork, though Calvin doubted he was actually reading any of it. The sun had dipped below the horizon, leaving the sky in that in-between state—dark enough for streetlights to flicker on, but still holding the last traces of daylight.

Calvin stared out the window, the city creeping back into focus. It was strange how normal everything looked when his entire world had just been upended. He had expected—what? That buildings would somehow look different now that he had signed himself into a shadowy government project? That the streets would feel less familiar?

"So, what's my story?" Calvin finally asked, breaking the silence.

Holt didn't glance away from the road. "Your new job is with a private defense contractor specializing in classified technology development. The company name is Evergreen Dynamics. It has a website, business records, and a solid cover."

Grayson added, "Your job title is Technical Analyst. If anyone asks what you do, it's IT security, system diagnostics, that kind of thing. Just enough to sound legit without raising questions."

Calvin exhaled. "Right. So, basically, my actual job, just with more lying."

Grayson smirked. "Exactly."

They pulled up outside his apartment, and Calvin hesitated before getting out. "So, uh, am I free to go about my normal life, or am I going to have you two lurking outside my door every night?"

Holt turned in his seat, finally meeting Calvin's eyes. "You're free to live your life as usual. But there will be check-ins. Don't talk about what you see. Don't do anything that will make us have to step in."

Grayson smiled slightly. "Enjoy your night, Mercer."

Calvin muttered something under his breath as he climbed out of the SUV, the weight of the last few hours hitting him all at once. By the time he got inside, his phone was already buzzing.

**Brandon.**

Calvin sighed before answering. "Yeah?"

"Dude, what the hell? You get taken by the Men in Black, and I don't hear from you for hours? What happened?"

Calvin took a deep breath. Time to test the cover story. "It was a job offer," he said casually. "Some defense contractor looking for people with my skill set. Apparently, I made some lists and got flagged as a good candidate."

Brandon scoffed. "A *defense contractor*? You fix laptops for old people. What, did they run out of qualified people at MIT?"

"Apparently, I have the right kind of experience," Calvin said, rubbing his forehead. "They do classified tech work. Can't really talk about it."

"Oh, come on," Brandon groaned. "You get offered some top-secret gig and you're just going to leave me hanging?"

"That's literally the point of 'top-secret,' Brandon."

His friend huffed. "So, does this mean you're quitting?"

"No, they're letting me keep my normal job. It's more of a consulting thing," Calvin said, already feeling exhausted by the half-truths. "I'll still be around."

Brandon was quiet for a moment. Then, "Well... damn. I was hoping this would be your supervillain origin story."

Calvin chuckled despite himself. "Not yet."

After hanging up, he tossed his phone on the bed and collapsed onto the mattress, staring at the ceiling. His mind wouldn't shut off. He kept replaying the day in his head—the meeting with Ellison, the NDA, the vague promises, the unsettling implications of what he'd signed up for.

What *was* this project? Why him? The government didn't just pluck random computer techs off the street. He didn't have the kind of background that screamed "top-secret candidate."

Was there something they weren't telling him? Of course there was. The real question was *how much* they weren't telling him.

He rolled onto his side, trying to force himself to sleep. But every time he closed his eyes, his brain conjured new theories. Was it advanced cyber warfare? AI development? Some next-level surveillance program? The words "temporal distress" from the NDA kept nagging at him, but he shoved the thought away. Too ridiculous.

But then again...

Calvin groaned and sat up, rubbing his face. It was going to be a long night.

And tomorrow, his real questions would begin.

# CHAPTER 5: NEW WHEELS, NEW LIFE

The alarm buzzed, jarring Calvin from the two hours of restless sleep he had managed to get. He groaned, rubbing his face as he forced himself upright. His body ached with exhaustion, but his mind was still running at full speed. The weight of the previous day still lingered—Ellison's vague explanations, the NDA, the feeling that he had stepped into something far beyond his understanding.

He trudged to the bathroom, splashed cold water on his face, and stared at his reflection. "Well, Mercer," he muttered, "you're either going to be a genius or an idiot for doing this."

Dressed and ready, he grabbed his bag and headed for the door, only to stop short when he spotted Holt and Grayson waiting outside.

"Morning, sunshine," Grayson greeted, tossing a set of keys toward him. Calvin caught them reflexively.

"What's this?"

"Your ride," Holt said flatly, nodding toward the curb.

Calvin turned his gaze to the sleek black sedan parked nearby. It was a government-issued vehicle, but it wasn't the standard forgettable fleet car. It had all the signs of high-end luxury—

smooth lines, tinted windows, an engine that probably purred like a content lion. Not too flashy, but clearly expensive.

Calvin let out a low whistle. "I was expecting a beater. Maybe something with 'PROPERTY OF THE U.S. GOVERNMENT' stamped on the side."

Grayson smirked. "We have standards."

Calvin clicked the unlock button, and the car responded with a soft beep. "Why aren't you guys driving me?"

Holt leaned against the railing. "We're not your chauffeurs, Mercer. You'll be driving yourself from now on. The GPS is pre-set with your destination."

Calvin sighed. "Great. Hope it doesn't drive me off a cliff."

He slid into the driver's seat, feeling the soft leather interior. The dashboard lit up, a crisp heads-up display glowing faintly. He barely had to touch the ignition before the engine hummed to life—smooth, powerful, a far cry from his aging Honda that rattled like a dying lawnmower.

As he pulled out of his parking spot, he glanced in the rearview mirror. Holt and Grayson were still standing there, watching him. Just a friendly reminder that he wasn't truly on his own.

The drive was easy. Too easy. Traffic seemed nonexistent, the lights all conveniently in his favor. Either this car had some next-level route optimization, or someone behind the scenes was clearing the way for him. He wasn't sure which thought unsettled him more.

He arrived at the facility's nondescript entrance, his car rolling up to a heavily secured gate. A small scanner flashed green, and the gate slid open without hesitation. As he pulled in, his stomach twisted in anticipation. This was it—his first real day at... whatever the hell this was.

A security guard directed him to a parking space, and as he stepped out, another official-looking man met him at the door.

"Mr. Mercer?"

"That's me," Calvin said, pocketing the keys.

"Follow me."

The interior of the building was as sterile as he remembered—cold walls, fluorescent lighting, the faint smell of industrial-grade air filtration. He was led through a series of hallways until they reached a large briefing room.

Inside, a half-dozen people sat around a conference table, engaged in quiet conversation. The moment Calvin stepped in, all eyes turned to him. He scanned the room, trying to get a read on them. They weren't what he expected—not that he even knew what to expect.

Some had the clean-cut look of military personnel, their posture rigid, their eyes assessing. Others looked more like academics, their clothes slightly disheveled, their expressions filled with curiosity. There was even a woman in a crisp medical coat, scrolling through something on a tablet.

Ellison stood at the head of the table. "Everyone, this is Calvin Mercer. He'll be joining the team."

Calvin offered a half-hearted wave. "Uh, hey."

A man with salt-and-pepper hair and a no-nonsense expression nodded. "Dr. Samuel Klein. Engineering and physics."

Next was a woman in her late thirties, wearing glasses and a sharp blazer. "Dr. Natalie Carter. Historical research and analysis."

An athletic-looking man, arms crossed over his chest. "Major Scott Reynolds. Tactical operations."

The woman in the medical coat looked up briefly. "Dr. Leah Voss. Medical and biological sciences."

A younger guy in a hoodie smirked. "Ethan Park. Cybersecurity and AI development."

Calvin blinked. "So... we have a physicist, a historian, a soldier, a doctor, and a hacker." He looked back at Ellison. "I hate to state the obvious, but what kind of job *is* this?"

Ellison smiled faintly. "The kind that requires a very particular mix of expertise."

Calvin looked around at the people in the room again. It still didn't make any sense. If this was just some advanced tech program, why the historian? Why the soldier? Why *him*?

His gut told him there was a much bigger picture he wasn't seeing yet. And he had a sinking feeling that by the time he did, it would be far too late to walk away.

# CHAPTER 6: THE UNSPOKEN TRUTH

C alvin sat in the conference room, hands resting in his lap, trying to look as composed as possible. In truth, his mind was still racing from the introductions. A historian, a soldier, a physicist, a doctor, and a hacker—what kind of project required all of them? What required him?

Ellison leaned forward, folding his hands neatly on the table. "Let's go around the room and get updates. We need to ensure everything is on track."

Calvin glanced around as the team members nodded in agreement. Whatever this was, they were already deep into it.

Ellison gestured toward Dr. Klein, the physicist. "Dr. Klein, let's start with you."

Klein cleared his throat, adjusting his glasses before speaking. "We've made progress refining the calculations. The last set of tests confirmed that the projection model holds under observed constraints. However, we're still dealing with stabilization issues. The energy requirements are... substantial."

Calvin frowned. Projection model? Stabilization issues? That sounded suspiciously like something beyond simple tech research. But before he could dwell on it, Dr. Carter, the historian, spoke up.

"My team has been working to refine the sequencing," Carter said, scrolling through a set of notes on her tablet. "We've narrowed down the key divergence points and confirmed that external variables remain stable up to the designated thresholds. If the next phase holds, we can proceed without additional recalibration."

Key divergence points? External variables? Calvin shifted in his seat. That sounded a hell of a lot like they were talking about... historical events.

Ellison nodded approvingly and turned to Major Reynolds. "And your team?"

Reynolds sat back in his chair, arms crossed. "We've conducted three new simulations since last week. Each one ended within an acceptable margin of error. The insertion and retrieval protocols have been refined, and our personnel are ready for live testing when given the green light."

Insertion and retrieval? Calvin swallowed. That sure as hell wasn't normal military terminology.

Ellison nodded, then looked at Dr. Voss, the medical expert. "Anything to report on your end?"

Dr. Voss tapped her pen against the table. "We're still refining the physiological impact models. The latest biometric readings are encouraging, but prolonged exposure to the field is causing elevated stress markers. There's a chance of long-term degradation if we don't introduce more safeguards."

Prolonged exposure? Degradation? Calvin's stomach twisted. They weren't talking about *field tests* in the normal sense.

Ethan Park, the hacker, was the last to speak. He leaned forward with an eager grin. "The interface is holding up. We managed to patch the synchronization lag, so the delay is almost negligible. Plus, we've reinforced the security protocols—there's no chance of external interference."

Synchronization? Security protocols? Calvin's fingers curled into a fist under the table. *They're talking about time travel.*

No one had said it outright, but it was obvious. The physicist was talking about stabilizing a projection model—probably some kind of time displacement. The historian was narrowing down "divergence points"—likely moments in history that could change. The soldier was running "simulations" and working on "insertion and retrieval." The doctor was worried about long-term exposure, and the hacker? The hacker had patched *synchronization* issues.

It all pointed to one thing.

But that was *impossible*.

Calvin forced himself to keep a neutral expression, but his mind was reeling. He had expected top-secret tech. Maybe weapons, maybe AI, maybe something along the lines of high-level encryption or cyber warfare. But *this*?

Time travel wasn't real. It was science fiction. Even if someone *did* figure out a way to do it, it would break everything science knew about reality. Wouldn't it?

He glanced around the room. No one else looked surprised. They were nodding along like this was just another day at work. As if any of this was *normal*.

Ellison finally turned toward Calvin. "Mr. Mercer, I imagine you have some questions."

Calvin blinked, realizing the room was now staring at him. He swallowed hard, forcing himself to sound composed. "Uh, yeah. A few."

Ellison gestured invitingly. "Go ahead."

Calvin glanced at Klein, Carter, Reynolds, Voss, and Park. Every one of them had contributed to what was clearly a massive undertaking. But what did they *think* he was here for? He wasn't a scientist. He wasn't a historian. He wasn't military.

"What exactly is my role here?" Calvin asked carefully.

Ellison smiled faintly. "We'll get to that soon."

Calvin narrowed his eyes. That wasn't an answer. That was *deflection*.

Before he could push further, Ellison stood. "Let's adjourn for now. Mr. Mercer, I'd like you to meet with me separately in my office. The rest of you, continue your preparations."

The team exchanged glances, then began gathering their notes. Calvin stayed seated, feeling the weight of the moment pressing down on him.

He wasn't crazy. He had heard what they said. They were talking about *time travel*.

And for some reason, he was now part of it.

# CHAPTER 7: THE PROBLEM WITH TIME

Calvin followed Ellison through a series of sterile hallways, his mind still racing from what had just transpired in the conference room. The pieces were all there, but his rational brain was screaming at him that it couldn't be real. He needed to hear it outright. He needed confirmation.

Ellison's office was as cold and minimalistic as the rest of the facility. A large desk sat neatly in the center, an array of monitors lining the back wall, each displaying incomprehensible data streams. No personal items, no decorations—just efficiency and order.

Ellison gestured to a chair across from his desk. "Have a seat, Mr. Mercer."

Calvin remained standing for a moment, then finally sat, rubbing his temples. "Alright. Just say it. You're talking about time travel."

Ellison's expression tightened, and for the first time, his composure seemed to falter. He exhaled slowly and gave a curt shake of his head. "We don't call it that."

Calvin raised an eyebrow. "Then what do you call it?"

Ellison folded his hands in front of him. "We refer

to it as **Temporal Displacement through Quantum Field Manipulation.**"

Calvin stared at him, deadpan. "So… time travel."

Ellison's jaw tensed slightly. "Time travel is an imprecise and misleading term. What we're working with is a controlled application of temporal physics, allowing for the selective relocation of matter across non-linear points in the space-time continuum."

Calvin let out a short laugh. "Yeah. Time travel."

Ellison sighed, but there was no amusement in his eyes. "You're here because we need your help, Mr. Mercer."

Calvin leaned back. "That's the part I still don't get. I'm a hardware guy. I fix circuits. I troubleshoot network issues. What part of that screams 'send this guy back in time'?"

Ellison didn't answer immediately. Instead, he stood, walked to a small console on the wall, and tapped a few commands. A large monitor flickered to life, displaying security footage of a sleek, metallic chamber with an array of monitoring equipment surrounding it. It looked like something out of a sci-fi movie.

"This," Ellison said, gesturing to the screen, "is our Temporal Displacement Chamber."

Calvin squinted at the image. "Okay. And?"

"We've managed to send objects forward in time. A few seconds, a few minutes. The problem," Ellison continued, his voice tight, "is what happens on reentry."

He tapped another button, and a different video appeared. The same chamber. A metal canister sat inside, surrounded by thick cables and an eerie blue glow. A countdown appeared on the screen. **3…2…1…**

The canister vanished.

Calvin's eyes widened. "Okay… that's impressive."

"Watch," Ellison said.

A few seconds passed. Then, with a sharp burst of energy, the canister *reappeared*—and immediately shot forward like a bullet, smashing against the reinforced wall of the chamber. The impact was violent, metal crumpling like a soda can. Whatever was inside was obliterated.

Calvin blinked. "Jesus."

Ellison nodded. "Every test so far ends the same way. Any object we send forward comes back at a velocity proportional to the energy of the displacement field."

Calvin exhaled, his brain shifting into problem-solving mode despite himself. "So, you're saying whatever comes back... comes back *fast*."

"Exactly," Ellison confirmed. "At the moment, it's the equivalent of dropping something out of a speeding car. The field disengages, and whatever returns to our time retains momentum. The farther we send something, the worse the effect."

Calvin frowned. "And I'm here because...?"

Ellison sat back down. "Because we need someone to solve it. Our teams have been working on theories, but we need a fresh perspective. Someone who thinks differently."

Calvin ran a hand through his hair. "And you think *I* can fix this?"

"You have an analytical mind, a strong background in electrical and mechanical engineering, and experience troubleshooting systems under unpredictable conditions. We need someone who isn't constrained by traditional academic approaches."

Calvin let out a breath. This was insane. A week ago, he was replacing laptop batteries. Now he was being asked to fix *time travel inertia problems*?

He shook his head. "This is nuts."

Ellison studied him carefully. "You signed on for something

bigger than yourself, Mr. Mercer. You *wanted* purpose. Here it is."

Calvin fell silent, staring at the frozen screen where the mangled canister remained embedded in the chamber wall.

Time travel—*temporal displacement*—was real.

And somehow, it was now his problem to fix.

# CHAPTER 8: THE HUNDREDTH FAILURE

The lab was a mess. Not in the chaotic, disorganized way of a hoarder's house, but in the hyper-focused, obsessive way that only came from pure, unrelenting frustration. Broken canisters—some dented, some crumpled, some flattened like roadkill—were strewn across the floor, forming an accidental graveyard of failed attempts. The smell of scorched metal and ionized air clung to everything, mixing with the stale scent of old coffee and sweat.

Calvin sat slumped over a console, his fingers rubbing his temples as he stared at yet another failed equation blinking on the screen. Across from him, Ethan Park, the cybersecurity and AI specialist, looked equally exhausted. His normally cocky smirk had faded days ago, replaced by an expression of resigned despair. His hoodie was wrinkled, his hair unkempt, and his bloodshot eyes were locked on the data readout, as if sheer willpower could force the numbers to change.

Park groaned, leaning back in his chair. "Cal, we've tried this a hundred times. Maybe it's not solvable."

Calvin exhaled sharply, his jaw tightening. "It's solvable. We're just missing something."

Park scoffed. "Missing something? We're missing *everything*. The math says the inertia has to go somewhere, but the field collapses before it can dissipate. Every time we send something, it snaps back like a goddamn rubber band on steroids." He gestured at the latest ruined canister lying in the testing chamber, its twisted remains still smoking. "How many more of these do we need to splatter against the wall before we admit defeat?"

Calvin ran a hand through his hair, staring at the data. He knew Park was frustrated. Hell, *he* was frustrated. Every idea they had tried resulted in the same problem—anything sent forward in time came back at breakneck speed, like it had been fired out of a railgun. If they couldn't figure out how to counteract the momentum, anything larger than a canister was going to be reduced to paste on impact.

Park sighed and rubbed his eyes. "Look, man. I know you don't want to hear this, but maybe time travel—"

"*Temporal displacement*," Calvin corrected automatically.

"Fine. *Temporal displacement* isn't meant to work like this. Maybe we've hit a fundamental wall of physics. Maybe the universe just says 'no' to anything staying gone longer than a few minutes."

Calvin shook his head. "No. That's not it."

Park leaned forward, resting his elbows on the console. "How do you know?"

"Because," Calvin said, eyes narrowing at the screen, "someone already figured it out."

Park frowned. "Says who?"

Calvin looked at him. "You really think they pulled together *this* team—historians, soldiers, physicists, medics—because they wanted to send tin cans into the future? No way. This project was built around a bigger idea. *Someone* knew this was possible, and now it's our job to make it work."

Park exhaled, shaking his head. "That's a lot of faith to put in classified government secrets."

"It's not faith," Calvin muttered, staring at the test logs. "It's pattern recognition."

Silence filled the lab for a moment, only interrupted by the hum of the equipment and the occasional flicker of a damaged light overhead. Calvin sat back, eyes scanning the data. There had to be something they weren't seeing, something fundamental about how the displacement field worked.

He glanced over at the chamber, at the latest wreckage inside. He had lost count of how many canisters they had destroyed. There was a sickening monotony to it now—set up the test, run the calculations, send the object forward, watch it come back as a pile of scrap. Rinse and repeat.

But *why* was it happening?

The momentum wasn't being absorbed. The field collapsed too fast. That much they knew. But how did *time* handle inertia? If an object moved through time, what was anchoring its relative speed? What was controlling its movement?

His fingers drummed against the desk, his mind circling the problem over and over.

"Alright," Calvin finally said, pushing his exhaustion aside. "Let's try it again."

Park let out an exasperated laugh. "Dude, you're seriously trying to break the definition of insanity right now."

Calvin ignored him. "Change the field parameters. Let's reduce the feedback threshold by half and reroute energy dispersal through the stabilization nodes."

Park hesitated, then sighed. "Fine. One more." He began typing commands into the console. "But if this one fails, I'm taking a nap. I don't care if the president himself walks through that door."

Calvin smirked. "Deal."

The chamber powered up, the blue glow intensifying as the system whirred to life. The latest test canister sat in the center, wires attached to monitoring sensors, its polished metal surface reflecting the harsh lab lighting.

Calvin exhaled, watching as Park input the final sequence. The countdown appeared on the screen.

**3...2...1...**

The canister *blinked* out of existence.

A few tense seconds passed. The readings scrolled across the monitor, streams of data processing the energy fluctuations, the field integrity.

Then, with a sudden burst, the canister *reappeared*.

And... it didn't slam into the wall.

It dropped, bouncing lightly onto the testing platform before rolling to a stop.

Calvin and Park stared at it, neither of them speaking.

"...Did that just—" Park started.

"It worked," Calvin whispered, barely believing it himself. Then, louder: "It *worked*."

Park let out a long, disbelieving laugh. "Holy shit. We didn't just fail for the hundredth time. We *won*."

Calvin's exhaustion was still there, but now it was overshadowed by something else—adrenaline, excitement, the thrill of actually solving something that seemed impossible.

He had cracked it. The first real step toward controlled time displacement.

And, somehow, he had the feeling that was just the beginning.

# CHAPTER 9: THE PARADOX APPEARS

The high-pitched hum of the lab's machinery had finally settled into something close to normal. The last test had worked. It worked. Calvin and Park had done it. But before they could celebrate too much, another canister *blinked* into existence on the testing bed with a faint crackle of displaced energy.

Park's head snapped toward it. His exhaustion was momentarily forgotten, his hands hovering over the keyboard. "Where the hell did that come from?"

Calvin, still riding the high of success, blinked at the newly arrived object, his brain trying to process what just happened. He slowly stood up from his chair, stepping toward the testing platform where the canister sat, looking identical to the one they had just sent.

"Oh great," Park muttered, rubbing his face. "We probably screwed something else up. Now we're going to be buried in an infinite loop of duplicate canisters popping out of nowhere."

Calvin didn't answer immediately. He knelt down, examining the canister. It was pristine, undamaged. Not like the crushed wreckage of their earlier failures. The same serial number, the same scuff mark on the side where he had accidentally brushed it against the worktable an hour ago.

Then it hit him. His stomach flipped as realization set in.

"No," Calvin said quietly. "We sent it."

Park frowned. "What? When?"

Calvin turned, eyes wide. "A few minutes from now." He stood up fully, turning back to Park with an urgency that sent a shiver down the hacker's spine. "Set up the field to send it back five minutes."

Park hesitated, looking between Calvin and the canister. "You're telling me that we *haven't* sent that yet?"

"Not yet," Calvin confirmed, his brain racing. "But we *will*."

Park let out a low whistle, dragging a hand down his face. "Dude, that's some real 'chicken or the egg' bullshit."

Calvin's heart was pounding. This wasn't just about solving the velocity issue anymore. This was different. This was... a paradox. The canister had arrived *before* they had sent it. That meant their experiment wasn't just *working*—it was creating a closed time loop.

He took a shaky breath, stepping back toward the console. "We need to do it, Park. If we don't, we break causality. It has to happen."

Park ran his fingers through his hair. "You're telling me that we have to send it back, because it already *has* been sent back?"

"Exactly," Calvin said, his voice firm. "If we don't, then how did it get here?"

Park let out an exasperated laugh. "Man, I did *not* sign up to become a walking paradox."

"None of us did," Calvin muttered, glancing again at the canister, which now felt far heavier than it had any right to be. It wasn't just an object anymore. It was proof that they had broken reality in a way no one had ever done before.

Park groaned, shaking his head. "Fine. But if this rips a hole in the universe, I am *not* taking the blame."

Calvin smirked. "Noted."

They worked quickly, setting up the displacement field again. Park punched in the parameters, hands moving a little faster than usual, as if some deep part of his brain was terrified of what they were doing.

Calvin took one last look at the canister, swallowing the lump in his throat. Then, he nodded. "Send it."

Park hit the key.

The chamber glowed. The air crackled. The canister shimmered —

And then it was gone.

Calvin and Park both stood in stunned silence, staring at the empty testing bed.

After a long moment, Park finally spoke. "Okay," he said slowly. "So, either we just confirmed the first stable time loop in human history… or we just broke everything."

Calvin let out a breath he hadn't realized he was holding. "I guess we'll find out."

Park laughed weakly, rubbing his hands down his face. "Man, I really need some sleep."

Calvin, however, couldn't stop staring at the empty space where the canister had been. Because for the first time, he wasn't just thinking about *how* they had solved the problem.

He was thinking about *who else had already done it before them.*

And that thought was far more terrifying.

# CHAPTER 10: PHASE TWO

Calvin stared at his phone for a long moment, hesitating. The lab around him was eerily silent now, except for the soft hum of cooling fans and the occasional beep from an idle console. Park had slumped into a chair, arms crossed over his chest, exhaustion finally winning the battle against adrenaline. But Calvin couldn't rest. Not now.

His thumb hovered over Ellison's contact. It was 3 a.m., and he had no doubt the director would be furious at being woken up by what he'd probably call a "couple of computer nerds" over a misplaced canister. But this wasn't just another glitch or failed test. This was **proof**. The paradox was real.

Screw it.

He pressed the call button.

The phone barely rang twice before a groggy but controlled voice answered. "Mercer, this better be good."

Calvin took a steadying breath. "We confirmed a closed-loop paradox, sir."

Silence.

Then Ellison's voice was sharp, awake. "Say that again."

"The canister showed up before we sent it. Five minutes before.

We verified the serial number. It's the same canister."

Another pause. Then, "I'm on my way."

Calvin let out a breath and ended the call. He turned to Park, who cracked one eye open. "We waking the whole circus up for this?"

"Ellison is. Get ready for a lot of pissed-off people."

Park groaned and stretched. "Fantastic."

---

Thirty minutes later, the lab was filled with a mix of excitement, irritation, and varying levels of sleep deprivation. The entire project team had been roused from their beds and dragged into the facility, some looking eager, others grumbling under their breath about being woken up by "a couple of computer nerds."

Dr. Klein, the physicist, rubbed his forehead, eyes bloodshot. "This had better be worth it."

Dr. Carter, the historian, on the other hand, looked intrigued. "A real paradox?" she mused, adjusting her glasses. "That's... groundbreaking."

Major Reynolds crossed his arms, unimpressed. "You called me out of bed for a **canister**?"

Ellison ignored the complaints, standing at the head of the room, his expression unreadable. "Mercer. Park. Show them."

Calvin stepped up, running his fingers through his hair before starting the demonstration. He and Park set up the field, explaining their breakthrough in counteracting the velocity issue and the moment the first paradox had appeared.

Then they ran the test again.

The team watched in silence as the canister blinked forward in time, vanished, and returned at a controlled rate. Then, after a pause, Calvin set the parameters to send it **back** five minutes.

And just like before, the moment they activated the field, a duplicate canister materialized on the testing bed before their eyes.

Silence.

For a long moment, no one spoke. No one moved. The weight of what they had just witnessed settled over the room like a suffocating fog.

Dr. Klein was the first to break the silence. He stepped forward, his voice lower than usual. "That's... That's not just theoretical anymore."

Dr. Voss, the medical expert, exhaled, shaking her head. "You just broke causality."

Reynolds, still skeptical, leaned closer to the testing bed and tapped the canister with his knuckle as if making sure it was real. "I don't like it."

Carter, on the other hand, grinned. "I love it."

Ellison let the murmurs continue for a few moments before raising a hand. The room fell silent. He turned to Calvin and Park, studying them both before speaking.

"We are now officially entering **Phase Two**."

Park's eyebrows shot up. "Wait. That wasn't Phase Two already?"

Ellison ignored him and turned back to the rest of the team. "From this moment forward, all previous assumptions are off the table. We now know controlled temporal displacement is viable. We now know paradoxes can be created and stabilized. That means we need to begin planning for the next stage immediately."

Calvin felt something sink in his chest. He thought this was it. He thought fixing the velocity issue was **his** job, and once that was done, he could step aside and let the real scientists and physicists handle the rest.

Apparently not.

Ellison met Calvin's gaze, as if reading his thoughts. "You solved the first major problem, Mercer. But you're not done. You're just getting started."

Calvin sighed and rubbed his face. "Of course I am."

Park clapped him on the back. "Look at it this way, Cal. At least we didn't break reality. Yet."

Calvin groaned. "Don't jinx it."

The rest of the team was already breaking off into their respective groups, debating next steps, throwing out ideas, recalibrating theories. The energy in the room had shifted. The project was no longer just an experiment.

It was real. And they were going deeper into the unknown.

Major Reynolds, however, remained unconvinced. He stood near the testing platform, arms crossed, a deep frown etched into his face. "This could be an error. A system glitch. Maybe your equipment is spitting out false readings."

Before Calvin could respond, another **canister** materialized onto the testing bed with the now-familiar crackle of displaced energy. The room went silent again, all eyes locking onto the impossible object.

Calvin felt his stomach drop. This one wasn't supposed to be there.

Park let out a low whistle. "Okay. Now that one *definitely* wasn't part of the plan."

Calvin slowly walked toward the testing bed, his heart pounding. He reached out, picking up the canister, turning it over in his hands. It looked the same as all the others, but something about this was different. This one… shouldn't exist. Not yet.

Then an idea struck him.

"Park, hand Major Reynolds a canister and a marker."

Park hesitated but did as he was told, grabbing a fresh canister and a black marker from the workstation and tossing them to Reynolds. The major caught both, giving Calvin a skeptical look. "What's this supposed to prove?"

Calvin held up the new arrival. "Write whatever you want on it and place it on the testing bed."

Reynolds narrowed his eyes, then uncapped the marker. With a deliberate motion, he scrawled something across the metal surface, shaking his head as he placed it onto the testing bed.

Calvin turned to Park. "Send it."

Park punched in the sequence and hit the activation key. The canister **blinked out of existence.**

At the exact same time, Calvin handed the earlier canister—the one that had appeared out of nowhere—back to Reynolds.

Reynolds turned it over and read the words written in his own handwriting:

**"This is Bullshit."**

The major's face paled slightly. His grip tightened on the canister, his entire body stiff as if he had just witnessed something he couldn't rationalize away.

The room was so quiet, Calvin could hear the distant hum of the ventilation system.

"Still think it's a glitch?" Calvin asked, raising an eyebrow.

Reynolds didn't answer immediately. He just stared at the canister, then at the now-empty space on the testing bed where it had originally arrived. Finally, he let out a slow breath and muttered, "Son of a bitch."

Ellison broke the silence. "I think that settles it."

The murmurs of the team grew louder, everyone exchanging theories, excitement, and unease. Calvin leaned against the workstation, watching the controlled chaos unfold. He thought about the implications of what they had just demonstrated.

They had just **proven** that information could be sent backward in time.

And for the first time, he fully grasped just how dangerous that could be.

# CHAPTER 11: NEEDLES AND SUSPICION

Calvin had just settled into his workspace when his phone buzzed. He glanced down and saw Ellison on the caller ID. A call from him was never good news. He answered cautiously. "Yeah?"

"Mercer, come to my office."

The line went dead.

Calvin sighed, rubbing his eyes before pushing himself up. He had barely recovered from last night's paradox demonstration, and now Ellison wanted something else? He trudged through the cold, sterile halls of the facility, past security checkpoints and empty corridors, until he reached the director's office.

Ellison was waiting for him, standing behind his desk, looking as composed as ever. The walls were lined with screens displaying scrolling data, but Calvin could never tell what any of it actually meant. The man gestured to the chair in front of his desk. "Sit."

Calvin sat. "This about last night?"

"No." Ellison leaned forward slightly. "You need to report to medical."

Calvin raised an eyebrow. "Uh… why?"

Ellison's expression was unreadable. "Your vaccines are not up to date."

Calvin frowned. "What? Why is that suddenly an issue now? I've been here for months."

"It's a requirement," Ellison said smoothly. "We have strict medical protocols in place. Everyone on this project is expected to be up to date on all required immunizations. It's non-negotiable."

Calvin studied Ellison's face. Something about this felt *off*. He had signed an absurd amount of paperwork when he started, but nobody had mentioned medical requirements before. If this was such a big deal, why hadn't they handled it during onboarding?

Calvin leaned back in his chair. "Didn't think experimental physicists needed a tetanus shot."

Ellison's lips pressed into a thin line. "Report to medical, Mercer. That's an order."

Calvin didn't like this. Not one bit. But he knew when arguing was pointless. "Fine."

---

After leaving Ellison's office, Calvin headed straight to **Park's** workstation in the tech lab. The hacker looked up from his console, mid-sip of an energy drink. "What's up?"

Calvin leaned on the desk. "Weird question—did they make you get vaccines when you started?"

Park frowned slightly. "Yeah, standard stuff. Why?"

"They're making me go now," Calvin said. "Months after I started."

Park tilted his head. "Huh. That is weird. Usually, they do that as part of onboarding."

Calvin exhaled through his nose. "Exactly."

"You think it's something else?" Park asked, lowering his drink.

Calvin shrugged. "I don't know. But I've got a bad feeling about it."

Park studied him for a moment, then nodded. "Watch your back."

Calvin nodded and turned toward the door. Whatever this was, it wasn't just about vaccines.

And he was going to find out why.

# CHAPTER 12: THE FIRST HUMAN TRIAL

The lab had never been this tense before.

For months, they had been running tests on inanimate objects, fine-tuning the calculations, ensuring stability. Then came the animal trials—first insects, then mice, and finally larger mammals. Each time, the results were the same: momentary displacement, no noticeable harm, but no true confirmation that a *human* could endure the process. Until now.

Ellison stood at the center of the room, his gaze scanning over the assembled staff. The entire team was present—Dr. Klein from physics, Dr. Carter from history, Major Reynolds from operations, Dr. Voss from medical, Park from cybernetics, and, of course, Calvin.

"This is it," Ellison said. "The next step."

Reynolds stepped forward. "We've selected multiple candidates from the team who have volunteered to go first. We'll begin with controlled, short-duration displacements. Three minutes forward."

The energy in the room was a mix of anticipation and anxiety. Calvin crossed his arms, shifting his weight from one foot to the other as he watched the first test subject—one of the junior researchers—step onto the pad. The man looked nervous, but determined.

The machine hummed to life, the containment field flickering around the test subject. Park monitored the system, his fingers flying over the keyboard. "Field stable. Energy dispersion normal. Ready for activation."

Ellison nodded. "Proceed."

Park pressed the key.

Nothing happened.

The machine powered down almost immediately, the energy field collapsing in an instant. The researcher was still standing on the pad, blinking in confusion.

Calvin frowned. "That's... not right."

Park checked the readings. "Everything was set correctly. The machine just... stopped."

Ellison's jaw tightened. "Run it again."

They tried another volunteer. Same result. The machine *started*—the energy ramped up—but then shut down before anything could happen.

Klein shook his head. "This doesn't make sense. The system should be working."

Frustration grew in the room. More volunteers stepped onto the pad. Each time, the machine refused to engage. It was as if *something* was preventing the process from initiating.

Calvin's mind raced. He watched as each attempt failed, his gut tightening with a feeling he couldn't explain. Then, without thinking, he stepped forward.

"I'll go," he said.

Every head in the room snapped toward him.

Ellison narrowed his eyes. "That's not necessary, Mercer."

Calvin ignored him and stepped onto the pad. "Something's

wrong. The machine won't start for anyone else. I want to see what happens."

Park hesitated. "Cal, I don't think—"

"Do it."

Ellison studied him for a long moment before finally giving a small nod. "Proceed."

Park swallowed hard and input the commands. "Alright... here goes." He pressed the activation key.

The hum of the machine deepened, the containment field glowing brighter than before. Calvin felt his skin tingle as the energy wrapped around him. A split second later—

The world vanished.

Then, just as suddenly, it snapped back into place.

Calvin staggered, nearly losing his balance as he found himself standing on the platform, gasping for breath. Every pair of eyes in the room was locked onto him in stunned silence.

Ellison's voice was barely above a whisper. "You disappeared."

Calvin blinked. "For how long?"

Park's eyes were wide. "Three minutes. Exactly three minutes."

Calvin's heart pounded. He looked down at his hands, then around at the team, their expressions a mix of shock, awe, and something else—something that felt unsettling.

He was the only one who had *gone through.*

And now, every single person in the room knew it.

Suddenly, the world blurred again.

Calvin gasped as he felt a rush of vertigo, his stomach flipping as the room flickered—

And he vanished.

A second later, he reappeared on the pad.

Shocked silence fell over the room.

Park's face went pale. "Where the hell did you go?"

Calvin swayed, gripping the edge of the console. "We sent me back five minutes."

Park's fingers froze over the keyboard. "But you disappeared before we sent you!!"

Dr. Klein took an unsteady step forward. "In theory… he can't be in the same place twice at the same time."

Park exhaled sharply. "Then how do we send him back?"

Calvin, still reeling, forced himself to stand straighter. "Send me back now."

Ellison hesitated, then gave a slow nod. "Do it."

Park reset the sequence, his hands shaking slightly. "This is either genius or incredibly stupid."

He pressed the activation key.

As soon as Calvin blinked out of existence—

He reappeared, not on the pad, but where he had been standing moments before his last disappearance. The second his feet touched the ground, his knees buckled, and he collapsed.

Then, without warning, he vomited onto the floor.

The team recoiled, the moment of scientific awe replaced by pure disgust. Dr. Voss immediately moved forward, crouching next to him as he heaved, his body shuddering. "Breathe, Mercer. In through your nose, out through your mouth."

Calvin coughed, wiping his mouth with the back of his hand. His face was pale, sweat beading at his brow. He looked up at the team, his vision swimming.

"Wow," he croaked. "That was **fucking weird**."

He swallowed hard, his stomach still twisting. "Let's not do that again."

Park muttered under his breath, "No argument there."

The room was silent again, but this time, the unease wasn't just from the experiment—it was from the realization that Calvin Mercer wasn't just *a* test subject.

He was *the* test subject.

And whatever was happening to him... it was only the beginning.

# CHAPTER 13: THE TRIP TO WASHINGTON

Calvin had barely finished washing the taste of bile from his mouth when his phone buzzed. He glanced at the screen.

**Ellison.**

Of course.

Still feeling lightheaded, he exhaled sharply and answered. "Yeah?"

"Come to my office," Ellison said, his tone flat as ever. "Now."

The line went dead.

Calvin muttered under his breath, pushing himself up from the bench outside the lab. His legs still felt wobbly from what had just happened, his stomach threatening to rebel again, but he steadied himself and started walking.

The halls of the facility were quiet, the air thick with that antiseptic smell that never seemed to fade. The further he walked, the more the unease in his gut twisted—not from the nausea, but from something deeper. Something was shifting, and he could feel it in his bones.

By the time he reached Ellison's office, he had already decided that whatever was about to happen, he wasn't going to like it.

Ellison sat behind his desk, his usual composed demeanor in place. He gestured to the chair across from him. "Sit."

Calvin slumped into the chair with an exhausted sigh. "If this is about me puking on your lab floor, I already feel bad about it."

Ellison ignored the comment. "Go home."

Calvin blinked. "Excuse me?"

"You need rest. Take a shower. Shave. Try on your new suit."

Calvin frowned. "I don't own a suit."

Ellison's lips curled into something resembling a smirk. "You do now."

Calvin's stomach twisted further. "Why?"

Ellison leaned forward slightly. "You're taking a trip to Washington."

The words hung in the air between them, thick and weighty. Calvin sat up straighter. "Washington *D.C.?*"

Ellison nodded. "You'll be meeting someone very important."

Calvin scoffed. "What, am I giving a TED Talk on how to vomit after time travel?"

Ellison didn't react. "You'll be meeting the President."

Calvin's breath caught. "The *President?*"

"Yes."

Calvin leaned back, running a hand through his hair. "Okay. Sure. That makes total sense. Because after almost turning myself inside out in a time travel experiment, the logical next step is a **trip to the White House.**"

Ellison simply folded his hands. "This was always going to happen. The timing just moved up."

Calvin narrowed his eyes. "Who else is coming?"

Ellison shook his head. "Just you and the agents."

Calvin frowned. "No scientists? No briefing team?"

Ellison gave him a measured look. "The President will explain the true reason you were hired."

Calvin's pulse spiked. "You mean you're *not* going to tell me?"

Ellison simply stood. "Go home, Mercer. Pack light."

Calvin pushed himself up, staring at the man. He had a hundred questions burning in his mind, but he already knew he wouldn't get any real answers here.

So, instead, he forced a smirk and muttered, "Guess I'd better go pick up my *brand-new* suit."

Ellison didn't smile. "It's waiting for you."

Calvin turned toward the door, his thoughts racing. The President. The *real* reason he was here. No briefing, no full team—just him.

Something was happening.

Something *big*.

And he had the sinking feeling that his life was about to change all over again.

# CHAPTER 14: WHEELS UP

Calvin woke to the sound of loud knocking at his apartment door. He groaned, rolling over to check the time on his phone. 4:30 a.m.

More knocking. Insistent.

With a sigh, he forced himself out of bed, still groggy, and shuffled toward the door. He cracked it open to find **Holt** and **Grayson** standing in the hallway, looking as sharp and unbothered as ever.

"Rise and shine, Mercer," Holt said, handing him a travel bag. "Time to go."

Calvin squinted at them. "Seriously? The President can't wait until the sun's up?"

Grayson smirked. "He's a busy guy."

Calvin sighed and rubbed his face. "Fine. Give me ten minutes."

"Five," Holt corrected.

Calvin grumbled but shut the door and threw on his newly acquired suit. It felt strange—far too formal for anything he was used to wearing. He ran a hand over his jaw, still clean-shaven from last night's shower, and took a long breath before stepping back out.

The drive to the airport was quiet, the early morning streets of Boston nearly empty. Calvin sat in the back of the black SUV, watching the city pass by, his mind still struggling to process everything that had happened in the past 24 hours.

When they reached the airport, they bypassed the main terminals entirely, pulling onto a private tarmac where a sleek, government-issued **Gulfstream jet** waited. The engines hummed softly, a few personnel moving about, preparing for departure.

Calvin whistled low. "Damn. Fancy."

Holt led the way up the stairs, and the three of them stepped into the cabin. The interior was luxurious but not excessive—polished wood paneling, leather seats, a small bar stocked with bottled water and coffee.

Calvin dropped into one of the seats, stretching out his legs. "I gotta say, I could get used to this."

Grayson smirked. "Don't."

The engines rumbled to life, and soon enough, they were airborne. The flight to Washington wasn't long—just over an hour—but it was quiet, the hum of the engines filling the silence. For the first time since he had met them, Holt and Grayson actually seemed... relaxed.

"So," Calvin said after a while, "what happens when I meet the President? Am I supposed to, like, bow or salute or something?"

Grayson chuckled. "It's not medieval times, Mercer. Just be respectful."

Holt added, "Address him as 'Mr. President.' Speak when spoken to. Keep it professional."

Calvin raised an eyebrow. "Right. Because I'm **known** for my professionalism."

Grayson smirked. "Hence the reminder."

Calvin sighed. "And what exactly am I walking into?"

Holt exchanged a glance with Grayson before answering. "That's above our pay grade. We're just making sure you get there in one piece."

Calvin frowned. That wasn't reassuring.

The rest of the flight passed in comfortable silence. The closer they got to Washington, the heavier the weight in Calvin's chest became. Whatever this was, whatever **he** was… it was bigger than he had ever imagined.

And soon, he was going to find out exactly **why.**

# CHAPTER 15: THE WEIGHT OF THE MISSION

The drive from the airport to the White House was as smooth and seamless as everything else had been so far. The streets of Washington, D.C. bustled with early morning activity, but Calvin barely noticed. His mind was too preoccupied, spinning with the weight of the unknown.

This wasn't a field trip. This wasn't a briefing. He was about to walk into the most secure building in the country and sit across from the President of the United States.

His stomach clenched as the SUV rolled through the White House gates. Agents stood at attention, their movements efficient and rehearsed. The vehicle came to a slow stop, and Holt turned toward him. "Time to go, Mercer."

Calvin took a deep breath, exhaling slowly. "Yeah. Sure."

He stepped out, straightening his suit, though it still felt strange on him. The weight of the moment pressed down harder with every step toward the entrance.

A staffer was already waiting. "Follow me."

Calvin didn't get much of a chance to take in his surroundings.

The hallways were a blur of polished floors, historic paintings, and an overwhelming sense of importance. Everything here had weight. Every step echoed through the halls of history.

Then, the doors opened, and he was ushered into the Oval Office.

The room was smaller than he expected, yet it radiated authority. Sunlight filtered through tall windows, casting long shadows across the polished Resolute Desk. And behind that desk sat **the President.**

Calvin swallowed hard.

"Mr. Mercer," the President said, standing and extending a hand.

Calvin hesitated just long enough to feel awkward before stepping forward and shaking it. "Uh, Mr. President."

The President gestured to the chair across from him. "Please, sit."

Calvin lowered himself into the chair, his back stiff. His pulse thundered in his ears. He wasn't sure what he had expected—maybe a whole team of advisors, generals, or scientists. But it was just him and the leader of the free world.

The President folded his hands on the desk and studied Calvin with a knowing expression. "I imagine you have a lot of questions."

Calvin let out a breath. "That's an understatement."

The President nodded. "Let me start with the most important thing you need to know: You are the only person who can time travel."

Calvin blinked. The words were so casually delivered that it took a moment to process them. "I—wait, what?"

"We don't know why," the President continued. "But before you were ever hired, we already knew that this would be the case. The past few months of testing were to confirm it."

Calvin felt a cold sensation creep into his spine. "How the hell did you know?"

The President's expression remained steady. "I can't tell you that."

Calvin clenched his fists against his knees. "Oh, great. That's reassuring."

"What I *can* tell you," the President said, leaning forward slightly, "is that your mission is critical. If you don't go back and ensure that the American Revolution unfolds exactly as it's supposed to, the United States will cease to exist."

Calvin's breath hitched. "What?"

"There are certain events—certain moments—that *have* to happen. If they don't, if history is altered even slightly, the country as we know it will never be formed."

Calvin shook his head, his pulse racing. "That's insane. How do you even know that?"

The President's gaze didn't waver. "Again, I can't tell you that."

Calvin felt like he was suffocating. His world, already spinning off its axis, was now flipping end over end. "So, what? You're just asking me to jump into the past and *wing it*?"

"No," the President said. "You will spend the next few months in intensive training. You'll learn the precise events you must protect. You'll be trained to speak, act, and live as if you belong in the 18th century. The weapons, tools, and supplies you'll need have already been prepared. You will be trained in their use."

Calvin exhaled slowly, his mind reeling. "And if I refuse?"

The President's expression darkened, but there was no malice in his voice—only cold certainty. He spread his arms wide. "Then all of this—" he gestured around the room, around the White House, around the very fabric of reality "—ceases to exist."

Calvin swallowed, the weight of the moment pressing down harder than ever. He was being asked to ensure that history unfolded as it was meant to. That the world he knew would remain intact.

His world.

His home.

His family.

The thought of losing it—of erasing *everything*—was too much.

He let out a slow breath and nodded. "Alright," he said, his voice steady despite the chaos in his mind. "I'll do it."

The President's gaze remained on him for a moment longer before he gave a small nod. "Good."

Calvin sat back in his chair, his mind swirling with everything he had just been told. But there was one question still burning inside him. He swallowed and asked, "Do I come home when my mission is complete?"

The President's face remained unreadable. "That will be up to you, Mr. Mercer."

Calvin frowned. "What does that mean?"

"We are working on a device that will return you home," the President explained. "I can't tell you it will work. We just don't know."

Calvin stared at him. "How does it work?"

The President exhaled and shook his head slightly. "I'm not a scientist, Mr. Mercer. That's a question for your team. They've been working on it for some time."

Calvin mumbled under his breath, "Secrets, in secrets, in secrets."

The President let out a small chuckle. "Welcome to Washington."

Calvin let out a slow breath. The enormity of it all weighed heavily on his shoulders. He had agreed to go.

But deep inside, he knew this was only the beginning.

# CHAPTER 16: THE TRAINING BEGINS

Calvin's world changed overnight. His clearance was upgraded to Top Secret/SCI, granting him unrestricted access to everything he needed to know. For the first time since being dragged into this project, there were no more vague answers or deflections. No more hidden truths.

If he asked a question, it was answered. He didn't always like the answers, but at least they were the truth.

His life before this—his old job, his apartment, his friends—was already fading from memory. The days blurred together, filled from morning to night with **training**.

He trained in **18th-century dialects and speech patterns**. His natural Boston accent wasn't far off, but there were subtle differences—phrases, idioms, and pronunciation quirks that could expose him instantly if he got them wrong.

He trained in **military tactics** of the era. **Muzzle-loading firearms**, **swordplay**, and even **bayonet drills**. Fighting in the 18th century wasn't about precision—it was brutal, chaotic, and up close. The thought of it made his stomach twist, but he knew he had to be ready.

He trained in **survival skills**, learning how to track, hunt, fish, and navigate without modern tools. How to cook simple meals over an open fire. How to sew his own clothes, mend his boots, and sharpen his weapons. He even learned how to **properly ride a horse**, a skill he never imagined needing.

He was also trained in **modern items disguised for the era**, tools that would give him an advantage but wouldn't stand out to the people of the time. These included:

- **A modern sniper rifle disguised as a musket** – Outwardly indistinguishable from an 18th-century flintlock rifle but with hidden internal components, allowing him to fire with modern accuracy and power when needed.

- **Hybrid Firearm:** A modern, precision rifle reengineered to look like a standard-issue musket. The exterior is refinished in period wood and metal, while hidden components (like its scope and firing mechanism) remain cloaked beneath the antique design.

- **Enhanced First Aid Satchel:** A compact kit filled with modern antibiotics, bandages, and sterilization tools, all stashed inside a leather medic's bag. To the casual observer, it appears to hold herbal remedies and rudimentary surgical tools typical of the era.

- **Binoculars designed to look like a simple spyglass** – A pair of high-tech digital binoculars concealed within a finely crafted brass spyglass. Its elegant engravings and weathered finish give it the look of a treasured antique, even as it offers modern optical clarity and night vision capabilities.

- **Inertial Digital Compass:** This self-contained sensor uses modern magnetometers and accelerometers to provide precise orientation without needing satellites, yet its appearance is entirely period-appropriate.

- **Concealed Multi-Tool Pocket Knife:** A modern multi-tool featuring items like a miniature screwdriver set, scissors, and a small cutting blade is hidden within the confines of a seemingly ordinary 18th-century pocket knife. Its outward simplicity masks a suite of modern survival tools.

- **A solar-powered emergency beacon concealed in a brass pocket watch** – His only link to the present, should extraction ever become necessary.

- **A boot knife made from advanced materials** – While small, it was nearly unbreakable and razor-sharp, disguised as a typical hunting blade of the time.

- **Fire-starting tools embedded in a flint and steel kit** – Ensuring he could start a fire in any condition without suspicion.

- **A lightweight, flexible body armor undergarment** – Designed to be worn beneath his period-appropriate clothing, offering some protection without detection.

- **Water Purification Device:** A compact, high-efficiency water filter is discreetly stored inside a small pouch that resembles a gunpowder bag. The pouch's period-accurate design—complete with wax seals and embossed motifs—makes it blend seamlessly with other Revolutionary-era accessories.

- **Compact Survival Rations:** Modern, high-calorie energy bars or freeze-dried meals can be packaged in small containers that mimic period storage methods—wrapped in parchment-like paper and tucked away in a discreet compartment of his travel bag.

But the most fascinating part—the part that made his pulse quicken—was the **history training**.

There were **five critical moments** that he had to ensure happened exactly as history recorded them. Some he had already known about from his lifelong fascination with history. Others...

Others challenged everything he thought he knew.

Some of what he was learning contradicted the **official historical record**. Small, seemingly insignificant details that, if altered, could change the course of the war.

This was **why he was here**.

**The Five Critical Moments:**

1. **The Boston Massacre (1770)** – Calvin must ensure that the tension between the British soldiers and the colonists escalates to violence. If the event is diffused, public outrage won't spread, and the revolution may never gain the traction it needs.

2. **The Midnight Ride of Paul Revere (1775)** – Revere must deliver his warning to the militia in time. While he was historically captured before reaching his final destination, other riders carried on the message. Calvin must ensure that the warning reaches its intended targets. Additionally, he must ensure that the first shot is fired at Lexington. Without it, the official start of the war could be delayed or derailed entirely.

3. **The Battle of Bunker Hill (1775)** – A strategic British victory that still galvanized the revolution. The colonists must hold long enough to inflict heavy British casualties before retreating. Calvin may need to ensure the famous order, *"Don't fire until you see the whites of their eyes,"* is actually given and followed.

4. **The Winter at Valley Forge (1777-78)** – A turning point for the Continental Army. If morale collapses,

Washington's forces could disband. Calvin must ensure that critical supplies reach the army, and that Washington maintains command and authority despite the hardships.

5. **Benedict Arnold's Betrayal (1780)** – If Arnold succeeds in handing over West Point to the British, the revolution could be crushed. Calvin must ensure Arnold's treachery is exposed before he can deliver the plans.

---

Each event was drilled into him. He was taught where to be, when to be there, and how to subtly influence the key figures involved. It wasn't about changing history—he was there to **make sure it stayed the same**.

However, he was also warned that **history is unpredictable**. His trainers made it clear—*there will be events no one foresaw, missions outside of your control.* He was told to **expect the unexpected** and be ready to **adapt on the fly**.

The weight of that responsibility settled deep in his chest.

Each night, exhausted, he collapsed onto his cot, his mind spinning with everything he had learned that day. And as much as he tried to ignore it, one thought kept creeping back.

The **President had never promised him a way home**.

And that terrified him more than anything else.

# CHAPTER 17: FINAL PREPARATIONS

The transformation was complete.

Calvin now **spoke only in period dialect**, his speech a seamless blend of 18th-century phrasing and cadence. His once-modern vocabulary was gone, replaced by formalities and expressions that felt so natural, he barely noticed the shift anymore. He no longer felt out of place speaking in the way of the time—he *was* a man of the 1770s now.

His wardrobe had changed as well. Every day, he wore **authentic period clothing**—a linen shirt, wool breeches, stockings, a waistcoat, and heavy leather boots. At first, it had felt strange, the layers cumbersome, the fabric itchy. But now? Now he barely thought about it. He moved in it like second nature.

Not everyone took it seriously.

"You know," Park smirked as he leaned against a lab table, arms crossed, "you're really committing to this whole *founding father cosplay* thing."

Dr. Klein chuckled as he walked past. "Aye, but dost thou find thyself *comfortable*, good sir?"

Calvin rolled his eyes but didn't break character. "'Tis a fine fit, and I do say, sir, better than any garb your sorry hide could fashion."

The room erupted in laughter.

"Okay, okay," Park held up his hands. "I take it back. That was impressive."

Calvin smirked. "One must commit fully, else one be lost."

But despite the ribbing, **they all knew it was necessary**. Every minute detail mattered. When he stepped through that machine, there would be no room for hesitation. No room for anachronisms. If he slipped up, even once, it could mean disaster.

## Final Checks

Calvin spent the next few days reviewing his **mission checklist**.

His weapons were packed, carefully hidden inside period-accurate containers. His musket, fitted with modern internals, was indistinguishable from any other weapon of the time. His **spyglass, first-aid kit, and knife**—all modified for secrecy—were secured in his satchel.

Dr. Voss had him run through **medical scenarios** one last time. "Remember," she reminded him, "infection was a death sentence back then. Use the antibiotics sparingly. If you get wounded, treat it in private—anything that heals too fast could make people suspicious."

Major Reynolds had him **drill his survival skills** one final time, making sure he could set up camp, clean game, and navigate the colonial terrain. "You might be in cities sometimes, Mercer, but don't count on it. You need to be comfortable living off the land."

His **historical training** had intensified. His instructors grilled him on **every major event, every important figure, and every key battle**. If someone asked him the name of the local blacksmith in a town, he had to know it. If they quizzed him on the politics of the time, he needed to be able to debate like a true revolutionary.

There was no more **training**.

It was time.

---

That evening, Calvin stood alone in his room, looking at himself in the mirror. The man staring back at him was no longer the bored technician who once spent his evenings watching history documentaries. He was someone else now.

Calvin **Mercer** was gone.

Who he had become... was about to be tested in the most extreme way possible.

Tomorrow, he would step into the past.

And history would be waiting.

# PART TWO

*Into the Past*

# CHAPTER 18: ARRIVAL IN THE UNKNOWN

Darkness.

Then, a crushing **weight**.

Calvin's senses flickered in and out, his body barely registering where—or when—he was. The last thing he remembered was standing in the lab, surrounded by the hum of machinery and the expectant faces of the team. Then came the pulse of energy, the world stretching and collapsing all at once, and then—nothing.

His mind felt like it had been wrung out and left to dry.

Slowly, reality crept back in.

The air smelled different—raw, **unfiltered**. Damp earth and fresh-cut grass filled his nostrils, unlike anything he had experienced in the sterile lab. The sound of rustling leaves, the distant chirp of birds—no hum of electricity, no voices, no machines. **Silence**, pure and uninterrupted.

He tried to move. Pain shot through his limbs—his body felt like it had been slammed against a wall. His fingers dug into the dirt beneath him, cold and damp. **Grass**. He was lying in a field.

His eyelids fluttered open, revealing a pale blue sky streaked with wisps of clouds. **No buildings. No roads. No signs of modern civilization.**

It worked.

He was in the past.

Panic flared in his chest as he pushed himself upright. His muscles screamed in protest, but he forced himself to move. **Where were his supplies?** He had been sent with enough gear to last months if necessary, but right now, all he saw was open land. He turned, scanning the area, and his breath caught.

Behind him, stacked neatly but partially covered in loose branches and dirt, were his supplies—crates of weapons, medical kits, food rations, period-accurate clothing, and a host of other carefully chosen equipment. **At least that part of the plan worked.**

He exhaled sharply. The team had chosen this **exact location** for a reason. The research had been meticulous—this field, in the mid-1770s, was **empty wilderness**, away from settlements. The perfect place to drop a man and a cache of anachronistic supplies without raising suspicion.

But he couldn't stay here.

If someone stumbled upon this stash, **everything** would be compromised.

His pulse steadied as his training kicked in. **First priority: hide the gear.**

He scanned the treeline in the distance. There—a rocky outcrop, partially covered in thick undergrowth. It would do for now.

Gritting his teeth, he forced himself to his feet. His knees wobbled, his head swam, but he pressed forward, dragging the first crate toward the makeshift cover. His fingers dug into the wooden edges as he hauled it into the brush, ignoring the sharp sting of blisters forming on his palms. **One by one**, he moved the crates, concealing them beneath a layer of fallen branches and dirt. **Temporary**, but it would buy him time.

By the time he was finished, his breath was ragged, sweat trickling down his back. He sank against a tree, chest heaving. **It was done.**

Now, the real challenge began.

He was alone, in a world where he did not belong.

And in a few short months, he would have to ensure the Boston Massacre happened exactly as history had recorded.

# CHAPTER 19: ESTABLISHING A COVER

The road was little more than a dirt path, uneven and lined with gnarled roots that threatened to trip him with every step. Calvin adjusted the strap of his satchel and kept walking, the weight of his concealed weapons and supplies pressing against his shoulder. The distant smoke of chimneys confirmed what he had hoped—he was near a settlement.

As he crested the hill, the town came into view. Wooden buildings, squat and functional, clustered around a central square. A few people milled about, some leading horses, others carrying goods. The air smelled of burning wood, damp earth, and something distinctly human—**unwashed bodies, livestock, and the sharp tang of tanned leather**.

He **had to blend in**.

Taking a steady breath, he adjusted his posture. He had rehearsed this countless times—**he was Caleb Mercer, a merchant's son from Barbados returning to Boston.** That story had to hold, no matter what.

Approaching a modest-looking **boarding house**, he took a moment to observe. The wooden sign creaked in the wind, its faded paint barely legible: **"Lodgings & Victuals - Mrs. Agnes Halloway, Proprietress."** A woman, well into her fifties, stood on the porch, watching him with the scrutiny of someone used to travelers.

Calvin mustered his best polite but weary smile and tipped his tricorn hat. "Good day, madam. I seek lodging for a time."

She narrowed her eyes, sizing him up. "And who might you be?"

He didn't hesitate. "Caleb Mercer, recently returned from my father's business in Barbados. I seek to establish myself in Boston."

A pause. Then, she nodded, apparently satisfied. "You've coin?"

He reached into his satchel and produced **a few Spanish reales**, common currency in the colonies. She inspected them, then nodded again. "A week in advance, and I'll not tolerate drunken fools nor bringers of trouble."

"I assure you, madam, I am neither."

She pocketed the coins and gestured toward the door. "Upstairs. Second room on the left."

---

## Laying Low & Planning Ahead

The room was sparse—a wooden bed, a basin of water, a small writing desk. The mattress was thin, filled with straw that smelled faintly musty, but it was a place to sleep.

Sitting on the edge of the bed, Calvin exhaled. **He was in.**

Now, he had to think ahead.

**The boarding house was a temporary solution**—he needed a permanent base of operations. Somewhere he could store his modern supplies without risk of discovery. A home of his own would be ideal, but purchasing property in 1770 wasn't as simple as handing over coin. He needed a **reason** to buy land.

For now, he had to establish his presence. He spent the next few days mingling, frequenting taverns and market stalls, speaking with merchants, sailors, and craftsmen—**learning who held influence and how trade moved through the town.** His cover as a young merchant fit perfectly; people were eager to discuss business, and it gave him an excuse to ask questions without drawing suspicion.

One evening, after earning the trust of a local merchant, he finally got the information he needed—a widow on the outskirts of town was looking to sell her late husband's home and land.

## The Safe House

The house was a modest structure, nestled near the woods, just far enough from prying eyes but close enough to the town to remain connected. **It was perfect.**

Negotiations were straightforward. Calvin, playing the role of a young man eager to settle down, paid generously. The widow, seeing no better prospects, accepted.

Over the next weeks, he transformed the house into **his base of operations**. Using his tools, he carved out **hidden compartments** beneath the floorboards, inside the hearth, and even within the walls—small caches where he could store weapons, modern medicines, and anything else that would be suspicious if found.

He even built a **concealed underground space**, accessible only through a false panel in the barn's foundation, large enough to store his **bulkier supplies**, including ammunition and long-term provisions.

By the time he was finished, the house was more than just a home—it was a **fortress of secrecy**, a safe house that even **British soldiers wouldn't be able to uncover if they searched.**

With his identity secure and his base established, Calvin finally allowed himself to breathe.

Now, he had one job.

**Ensure history remained intact.**

The Boston Massacre was only months away. And he had work to do.

# CHAPTER 20: THE STREETS OF BOSTON

Calvin had seen Boston before—modern Boston, with its packed streets, historic landmarks nestled between glass skyscrapers, and the hum of twenty-first-century life. But this Boston was something entirely different.

As his horse-drawn wagon crested the last rise before town, he took in the sight of a city that was both **familiar and utterly foreign**. The layout was largely the same—narrow, winding roads leading to the heart of the town—but there were **glaring differences**. The **Back Bay was still a bay**, not yet filled in for expansion. Beacon Hill and Dorchester were **actual hills**, not the flattened remnants he knew. Wooden wharves jutted into the harbor, and ships, their sails taut in the wind, crowded the waterfront.

And the smell—**salt air mixed with manure, wood smoke, and unwashed bodies**—hit him like a punch to the gut. Boston in 1770 was **alive in a way that modern Boston could never be**.

He guided his horse toward the town center, keeping his expression neutral as he scanned the streets. This was reconnaissance—his first real chance to get the temperature of the place. **How restless were the people? Was the revolution already simmering?**

He passed merchants peddling fish, bakers shouting about fresh bread, and clusters of **British redcoats** patrolling the streets, muskets slung over their shoulders. His gut tensed at the sight of them. They were younger than he had imagined—**boys, really**—some laughing, others looking bored.

But the **townspeople were wary**. He saw the glances, the way people stepped just slightly out of the way, not out of deference, but out of thinly veiled irritation. **Tensions were there, just beneath the surface.**

## Blending In

Calvin pulled the wagon to a stop outside a bustling tavern, one of many along the main thoroughfare. The **Green Dragon Tavern—a known meeting place for revolutionaries, even if it wasn't yet at full capacity as a resistance hub.**

He stepped down from the wagon, dusting off his coat, and tied his horse to a post. As he walked toward the door, he caught his reflection in a glass window. **He looked the part now—his hair slightly longer, his coat worn enough to seem traveled, his boots scuffed from miles on dirt roads.** He had spent weeks in his cover, and now it had to hold up under scrutiny.

Inside, the air was thick with **smoke, ale, and sweat**. The murmur of voices filled the space as men gathered in small clusters, drinking, talking. Some **argued politics**, others **complained about taxes and British rule**. He took a seat at the bar, casually listening.

"What'll you have?" the barkeep asked, eyeing him with the mild curiosity of someone who had seen thousands of travelers come and go.

"Ale," Calvin said, sliding a coin across the wood. "And perhaps some conversation."

The barkeep smirked. "Depends on what kind of conversation."

Calvin leaned in slightly. "I hear the mood in Boston is shifting.

Trade is tight. The Crown is pressing harder."

The man snorted. "Aye, and you'll find no love for His Majesty in this room. The **Lobsterbacks**"—he nodded toward the street—"act like they own the place. A man speaks against 'em, and suddenly, he's a traitor. I tell you, it's like a powder keg ready to blow."

Calvin nodded thoughtfully. **Good. The tension was already here. He wouldn't have to push too hard to set things in motion.**

---

## A Place to Stay

Over the next two days, he explored the city, keeping his questions subtle. He stopped by the docks, listening to the complaints of merchants frustrated by British tariffs. He wandered through the markets, noting which goods were becoming scarce. He **watched the British troops**, learning their patrol routes, their numbers, their weaknesses.

But he needed a **place to stay**—a reason to be in Boston without drawing suspicion.

On the third day, he found it. A small, two-story **rented room above a tailor's shop**, just enough space for him to maintain a presence in the city without committing too much attention to himself. He paid the owner a fair price, keeping his explanation simple.

"Trade between the islands and the colonies is uncertain," he explained. "I need to keep my ear to the ground."

The tailor, a middle-aged man with a shrewd look, accepted the money without argument. "Aye, well, times are uncertain for all of us."

With that, **Calvin had his foothold in Boston.**

Now, all he had to do was **ensure the first spark of revolution caught flame.**

## The Boston Massacre was just **weeks away.**

# CHAPTER 21: THE GREEN DRAGON

The tea was bitter, as always. No matter how many months he had spent in this time, Calvin still hated it. He scowled slightly as he took a sip, the warmth doing nothing to improve the taste.

**Typical American**, he mused. It was almost amusing that he had been trained in so many things—how to fire a musket, how to ride a horse in the style of the time, how to blend in seamlessly—but no one had ever trained his taste buds. He longed for a strong, **hot coffee**.

He sighed, muttering to himself, **"I wish I could get a decent coffee."**

"You say coffee?"

Calvin's heart **lurched** as he realized someone had overheard him. He turned slightly to see a man standing nearby, his expression one of mild curiosity. **Damn it.** He had let his guard down. He had to recover—fast.

He forced an easy smile, leaning back in his chair as if the thought had been idle conversation. "Aye," he said, adjusting his accent into something more casual. "Developed a taste for it while traveling with my father's company. The islands, mostly."

The man raised an eyebrow, intrigued. "You've been to the islands?"

Calvin nodded, thankful for the backstory he had crafted. "My father was in trade. Spent years around the Caribbean, down in Jamaica, Barbados." He shrugged. "Coffee's common there. Easier to come by than tea, in fact."

The man grinned. "You'd do well at **the Green Dragon Tavern, then**."

Calvin blinked. "They serve coffee?"

"Aye, that they do. Not many places in town do, but the Dragon sees a fair bit of trade from men who've been to sea and **don't care for English tastes**."

It made sense. The Green Dragon had always been known as a **gathering place for revolutionaries**—tradesmen, dock workers, and those dissatisfied with British rule. It would be a **perfect** place to spend time, listen, and observe.

Calvin thanked the man and made a mental note. **The Green Dragon. It was time to make it his new haunt.**

---

**A Familiar Crowd**

Days later, Calvin found himself seated at a corner table in the Green Dragon, the **smoky air thick with the scent of pipe tobacco, ale, and roasting meat**. The tavern was lively, filled with **merchants, sailors, and craftsmen**—men with **strong opinions and quick tempers**.

The first time he had stepped inside, he had simply listened, sipping the long-awaited coffee he had craved. But tonight, something was different.

As he scanned the room, his breath **caught in his throat**.

He knew **those faces**.

Not just from history books, but from **portraits, currency, statues. Samuel Adams. John Hancock. Paul Revere. James

**Otis.**

They weren't sitting together, but he could see them spread across the room, speaking in hushed tones with various groups. This wasn't just a gathering of merchants—**this was a meeting of men who would soon shape the course of history.**

Calvin took a slow sip of his coffee, forcing himself to stay casual. He had spent **his entire life reading about these men**, and now they were right in front of him.

He had to be careful. **He couldn't just approach them outright**—not without reason, not without raising questions.

Instead, he selected a **table close enough to hear, but not so close as to be obvious**. He had to **find a way into their good graces**, but he also couldn't get too involved. If he became too central to history, it could change everything.

It was a delicate balance.

He took another sip, heart pounding as he listened to the murmurs around him. If he played his cards right, **he would earn their trust.**

And from there, he could ensure that history remained intact.

# CHAPTER 22: A NAME TO WATCH

C alvin no longer sat alone at the Green Dragon. The faces around him had become familiar, the conversations easy. He had become a known presence, an affable merchant's son with a keen ear for business and a knack for friendly conversation. He never pushed too hard, never asked too many questions—but he listened, and he was remembered.
He had won trust, but time was running short.

The Boston Massacre was only days away, and he had to ensure it happened.

He had yet to determine exactly how he would make sure that **one fight on King Street ignited the flames of revolution**, but he knew the name **Edward Garrick**. The teenage boy was the matchstick that would set the night ablaze.

Calvin didn't have to wait long.

One afternoon, while sharing a drink with a group of regulars, the tavern door swung open, and a young boy stepped inside. The boy's name caught Calvin's attention first.

"Edward Garrick," the older man said, clapping the boy on the back. "Come in, lad."

Calvin's mind raced. Edward Garrick. **That** Edward Garrick? He hadn't expected to stumble upon him so easily. He took a steadying breath, forcing himself to remain casual. He forced himself to remain casual as the boy approached a man at the table.

Calvin's breath caught for just a second, recognition jolting him. He forced himself to remain casual as the boy approached a man at the table.

"Mr. Fielding, I came as you asked."

The older man, a portly leatherworker, nodded. "Aye, lad. Sit a moment." He gestured to the empty seat beside him, and Edward obeyed, looking eager.

Calvin leaned back, nursing his drink, careful to seem uninterested. **He had to keep tabs on the boy.**

As the conversation at the table carried on, Calvin engaged in casual discussion but listened keenly whenever **Edward spoke**. The boy was **sharp-tongued and full of bravado**, speaking with an air of self-importance that only the young could pull off. He prided himself on knowing the goings-on of Boston, eager to prove himself among the men.

It would only take **one well-placed insult**, one **spark**, to set the riot in motion. And **it had to happen soon.**

As Edward got up to leave, Calvin made sure to catch his eye. "Boy," he said casually, "how's business at Mr. Piemont's wig shop?"

Edward blinked, momentarily surprised that Calvin knew of his workplace. Then he straightened, grinning. "Busy as ever. The redcoats always want their wigs powdered and styled, even when they've nothing better to do than parade about."

Calvin chuckled. "A waste of good powder, if you ask me."

Edward grinned wider and nodded. "That it is."

And just like that, **Calvin had opened a door.**

Now, he had to wait for the moment history required.

# CHAPTER 23: THE SPARK OF A REVOLUTION

March 5, 1770

The tension in Boston had been rising for weeks, and Calvin could feel it in the air, thick as the smoke that curled from the tavern hearth. He sat at his usual spot in the **Green Dragon Tavern**, his fingers loosely wrapped around a mug of ale, but his mind was elsewhere. **This was the day.**

Edward Garrick sat at a nearby table with a few other apprentices, all of them young, brash, and well into their drinks. The boys laughed loudly, oblivious to the storm that Calvin knew was about to break. **Thirteen years old and drinking like grown men.** The thought made Calvin grimace, but this was the world he lived in now.

He watched the boy carefully, waiting for the right moment. It wasn't long before Edward, his face flushed with alcohol and youthful arrogance, started running his mouth. The moment was near.

Calvin turned to the man seated beside him, a leatherworker

named **Daniel Kent**, making sure his voice carried just enough. "I heard that redcoat Captain-Lieutenant John Goldfinch say the wig he bought was poor quality," he said, his tone casual. "And that he wasn't going to pay for it."

Across the room, Edward stopped mid-laugh.

Calvin didn't look at him, didn't acknowledge him at all, but he could **feel** the boy's attention snap to the conversation. His jaw tightened as guilt clawed at his stomach. **This is wrong. He's just a boy.** But history had to happen.

"That bastard," Edward muttered, shoving his drink aside.

His friends smirked. "What's the matter, Eddie? You going to go demand your coin from a soldier?"

Edward stood up sharply, wobbling slightly before finding his balance. "Aye," he spat, "that redcoat's going to learn that Boston men don't work for free."

Calvin forced himself to remain seated as Edward stormed out of the tavern, his friends trailing after him. His heart pounded against his ribs. **He had done it.** But at what cost?

# CHAPTER 24: THE FIRST SHOT

Calvin followed at a distance, keeping his head low as he wound through the streets toward King Street. The night was cold, the air sharp in his lungs, but the streets were alive—the scent of damp wood, horse dung, and the faint salt of the harbor mixed with the rising voices of an agitated city.

Edward and his friends had already reached **Private Hugh White**, who stood at his post outside the **Custom House**. Calvin ducked into the shadows of a nearby building, his breath coming shallow as he took in the scene.

Edward, red-faced and angry, squared up to **Captain-Lieutenant John Goldfinch**, jabbing a finger toward him. "You think you can cheat honest men out of their coin?"

Goldfinch didn't even glance at him. **He had already paid.** He had no reason to engage with a drunken boy.

But Private White did.

"Mind your tongue, boy," White snapped, stepping forward, musket in hand.

Edward's hand curled into fists. "Or what? You'll run me through?"

White moved quickly, **striking the boy across the side of the** head with the butt of his musket.

Edward **cried out**, stumbling backward, hands clutching his temple. His friend, **Bartholomew Broaders**, rushed forward, shoving White's chest.

Calvin's stomach **twisted. It was happening.**

People began gathering, their voices rising in outrage. **The bells of nearby churches began to ring—a fire alarm—but there was no fire tonight.** More Bostonians poured into the streets, drawn by the sound, by the growing shouts of anger.

White took a step back, suddenly realizing he was **alone** against a growing mob. Calvin could see the panic in his eyes. He reached the steps of the Custom House and called for reinforcements.

Minutes later, **Captain Thomas Preston arrived**, leading **six redcoats with bayonets fixed**. They formed a semicircle around White, muskets raised, trying to push back the crowd.

The mob only grew louder, more aggressive.

Calvin forced himself to **breathe**, his pulse hammering in his ears. **They weren't going to fire.**

Henry Knox, a young bookseller, stepped toward Preston, his voice calm but firm. "If your men fire, Captain, you must die for it."

Preston's face was set in stone. "I am aware of it."

Calvin swallowed hard. **This was the moment.** But there was hesitation, uncertainty.

The soldiers weren't firing.

Calvin looked down. Snow and ice littered the street, the remnants of a cold winter. **One push. One last push.**

His fingers curled around a chunk of ice, his muscles tensing. He lifted it, exhaling as he hurled it forward.

The ice struck **Private Montgomery**, knocking him off balance. **His musket fired.**

Silence. Then—

A crack of gunfire tore through the air.

Screams. More shots. Chaos.

Calvin stood frozen, watching the blood spill onto the snow. **He had done it.**

History had been written in gunpowder and blood.

Gunpowder smoke lingered in the air, mixing with the crisp winter cold. The scent of blood, sweat, and fear filled Calvin's nostrils as the echoes of the last shot faded into a stunned silence.

He stood frozen, his mind racing, his body refusing to move. The street before him was a tableau of **history in motion**—a chaotic, living nightmare. **The bodies on the ground were no longer names in a book. They were men.**

**Crispus Attucks** lay sprawled in the snow, his lifeless eyes staring at the night sky, his body still as the blood pooled beneath him.

Samuel Gray, a rope maker, had fallen to his knees before slumping onto his side, a dark red stain spreading across his chest. **James Caldwell**, a sailor, was slumped against a wall, mouth open as if he had tried to take one last breath before death took him.

**Samuel Maverick**, just **seventeen years old**, had staggered back before collapsing, a stray musket ball having found him in the chaos.

And **Patrick Carr**, groaning in pain, had fallen but was still alive, though his breathing was ragged, shallow. He wouldn't make it. **He was already as good as dead.**

Calvin's mind recited their names like a curse. **He knew them. He knew what they had done, what they would have done, what their deaths would mean.** But none of that mattered in this moment, because right now, he wasn't standing in a history book.

He was standing in the middle of a massacre.

The crowd had scattered after the gunfire, some frozen in shock, others running in fear. The survivors who remained stood in a horrified daze, staring at the blood-slicked cobblestones. Some wailed, others cursed the soldiers, and some simply watched in silence, trying to comprehend what had just happened.

The **redcoats**, too, seemed paralyzed. Private Montgomery still held his musket tightly, his breath coming in rapid gasps, his face white as the snow around him. **None of them had meant for this to happen.**

Captain Preston stepped forward, his voice tight but firm. "Hold your ground! Do not fire again!"

Calvin's chest **tightened**, his breath shallow. He wanted to move, to step back, to disappear into the shadows, but his legs wouldn't obey. **He had thrown that ice. He had started this.**

A dull ringing filled his ears, drowning out the shouts of the crowd. He could hear his own pulse, pounding like war drums in his skull. **History had to happen. This had to happen. But that didn't make it right.**

He looked down at his hands, fingers trembling. He hadn't fired a weapon. **But had he just killed five men?**

A movement to his right startled him. A woman had fallen to her knees beside Crispus Attucks' body, her hands covering her mouth in horror. Another man crouched beside Patrick Carr, pressing a hand to the wounded man's chest, whispering desperate reassurances. **Futile words.**

Calvin swallowed, forcing his legs to move. He had to get out of here. He had done what he came to do. But as he turned, he locked eyes with **Henry Knox**—the bookseller, the future general, a man who would help shape the Revolution. Knox's face was pale, his lips pressed into a hard line.

He had seen Calvin standing there. Watching. Not reacting like the others. **Had he noticed? Had he sensed something was off?**

Calvin forced his expression into something blank, something unreadable, before nodding slightly and turning into the crowd. He pushed past stunned bystanders, stepping over patches of bloodstained snow, his pulse hammering in his ears. He needed to get back to the Green Dragon. He needed to be away from here before someone started asking questions.

Because in this moment, he didn't feel like a historian. Or a patriot.

He felt like a murderer.

# CHAPTER 25: THE PRICE OF JUSTICE

The Green Dragon was quieter than usual, the usual rowdy tavern-goers subdued. The massacre had changed the city overnight—Boston was a powder keg, waiting for a spark. The anger on the streets was palpable, and the British soldiers were now the most hated men in the colonies. Calvin had known this would happen, had read about it, but living it was an entirely different experience.

He sat at his usual table, slowly turning his mug of ale between his fingers, staring into the dark liquid like it held answers. His stomach twisted with guilt, but **he couldn't allow himself to wallow in it**. There was still **work to be done**.

The British soldiers who fired on the crowd had been arrested, and the colony was demanding **blood**. The king had abandoned them, refusing to intervene. They were alone. The people wanted justice—**justice in the form of a hanging**.

That was not how this had to happen.

Across the room, **John Adams and Samuel Adams sat in a heated discussion**, their hushed voices carrying enough urgency that Calvin could feel the tension. Sam was **furious**, his face red as he gestured wildly, slamming his palm against the table.

"You cannot be serious, John," Sam seethed. "You would defend **them**? The very men who murdered our citizens?"

John sighed, rubbing his temple. "They are entitled to a fair trial, Sam. That is the law."

Sam scoffed. "The law? Whose law? The law of the tyrants who **stationed an army in our streets**?"

Calvin knew this was **the moment**. If John Adams didn't defend the soldiers, history could **veer off course**.

He leaned forward, setting his mug down with a deliberate **thud**. "John is right," he said calmly.

Both Adamses turned toward him, startled. They hadn't noticed him there. Sam's eyes narrowed. "And who are you to weigh in?"

Calvin offered a slight shrug. "A simple merchant." He nodded toward John. "But he is right. If we wish to prove that **we are better than the Crown, that this colony is not ruled by emotion but by law, then those soldiers must stand trial.** And they must be given a fair one."

Sam shook his head, his frustration mounting. "Fair? Tell that to the **widows of the men they killed**!"

John, however, was studying Calvin carefully. "You believe this is necessary?"

Calvin held his gaze. "I do. If we are to build something greater than the British, something that will **stand the test of time**, then our justice must be different from theirs." He took a slow breath. "Or would you rather we become the very tyrants we claim to despise?"

Sam's mouth opened, but no words came. He was angry, but he couldn't refute the logic.

John, however, nodded slowly, the decision settling over him. "I will defend them."

Calvin let out the breath he hadn't realized he was holding.

Sam ran a hand down his face, exhaling sharply. "I hope you know what you're doing, John. This could ruin you."

John smiled faintly. "Then so be it."

The conversation shifted slightly, but the Adamses kept stealing glances at Calvin. Finally, Sam spoke. "Your accent… it is not entirely of Boston."

Calvin smiled, leaning back. "My father was a merchant. I was raised in the **Caribbean**, spent time in **many ports**. It rubs off on a man."

John gave him a long, measuring look. "You are a peculiar sort, Mr. Mercer."

"I'm just a merchant," Calvin said with an easy grin. "And I wish to stay that way."

But inside, he knew. **They had taken notice of him.** And history was far from done with him yet.

# CHAPTER 26: THE LONG ROAD TO LEXINGTON

John Adams had done what Calvin had nudged him toward—he had defended the British soldiers. Against the full fury of Boston's citizens, Adams had stood firm, insisting that law must be upheld, and in the end, he had succeeded. The trial had ended with acquittals for most of the soldiers, with only two convicted of manslaughter rather than murder. The decision had not been popular, and Adams had been called a traitor by many. But Calvin knew—this was the moment that solidified Adams as a man of principle, someone the future nation could trust.

But there was no time for Calvin to dwell on that. **Five years remained until the next crucial moment in history—Paul Revere's midnight ride and the battle of Lexington.** The Revolution had many steps before the first real shots of war. Some of those moments, he would **watch from the shadows**. Others, he would have to **step forward and make sure history stayed on course.**

In the years since the massacre, Calvin had **woven himself into Boston's merchant class**, carefully walking the tightrope between **gaining influence and remaining unseen in history.** He had **built relationships**, gained the trust of **key members of the Sons of Liberty**, and even **made himself a small fortune**, almost by accident. Acting as a merchant had started as a cover, but he had found himself **exceptionally good at it**—importing and trading in textiles, glassware, and small goods while keeping an ear on the whispers of revolution. His role gave him access to conversations and connections that **no mere observer should have**.

One such event came **on a cold December evening in 1773**—the night of the **Boston Tea Party**.

The streets of Boston were tense, filled with whispers and quiet urgency. The docks, usually bustling with trade, had become a battleground of **resentment and defiance**. The Tea Act had pushed the colonists too far. **Three ships sat in the harbor, their holds filled with chests of British tea.** Tonight, those chests would never see a single coin in payment.

Calvin moved among the gathered men, listening, observing. **They weren't dressed as Mohawk warriors—not really.** That had been a myth that modern history had exaggerated. Instead, most of them wore **their everyday clothes, their faces hastily smeared with soot or paint, a few feathers tucked into their hats.** It wasn't about disguising themselves as Native Americans —it was about **symbolism**. They weren't trying to place blame elsewhere. **They wanted the British to know exactly who had done this—but no specific individual could be held accountable.**

Calvin pulled his cloak tighter around himself, watching as **Samuel Adams** raised his voice to the restless crowd. "Tonight, we stand as free men! The Crown would have us kneel, but we shall make it clear—we will not drink their **damned tea!**"

A roar of agreement surged through the assembled men.

Calvin smirked as he stepped beside Sam, lowering his voice. "And I suppose this means you'll be switching to coffee, then?"

Sam let out a hearty laugh, clapping Calvin on the back. "Aye, I suppose we all shall! I hope you're pleased with yourself, Mercer. You may have just changed the drinking habits of an entire nation."

Calvin chuckled, shaking his head. "Stranger things have happened."

He mused internally, glancing at Sam. Part of his merchant trade had included **importing coffee beans**—not a major product, but one he had noticed **slowly gaining popularity** among certain groups. And now, with British tea about to be dumped into the harbor and boycotted across the colonies, he had a feeling that demand for coffee was about to explode. **Unintentionally, he might have just positioned himself ahead of a coming trend.**

The plan was simple: **board the ships, break open the tea chests, and dump them into the harbor. No looting. No burning. No harming the crew.** This was not a riot—it was a message.

Calvin moved with the others, grabbing hold of a crate and heaving it onto the railing. His fingers **tightened** as he pried it open, revealing the **tightly packed bricks of tea leaves** inside. For a moment, he hesitated.

**In his time, this was a legend. Now, it was real. And he was a part of it.**

A man beside him grinned. "No time to hesitate, friend! Let's send this damned tea back to the sea where it belongs!"

Calvin nodded, swallowing his awe, and helped toss the crate into the water below. Around him, dozens of others did the same. The dark waters of Boston Harbor **turned brown with tea**, the scent rising into the winter air.

A strange **exhilaration** filled Calvin. He wasn't just watching history—**he was living it.**

But he had to remember his place. He was an **observer**, a guardian of the past. And his true mission was still years ahead.

As the last crate splashed into the harbor, Calvin exhaled. **One event down. Many more to go.**

# CHAPTER 27: THE RISING STORM

The years following the Boston Tea Party had been a slow but steady march toward open rebellion. Calvin had watched the British response unfold, each act of oppression tightening the noose around the colonies. The Intolerable Acts had pushed the people of Boston to their breaking point. The port had been closed, choking the city's economy, and British soldiers patrolled the streets with an air of dangerous authority.

Calvin had spent the time **expanding his network**, trading not just in goods, but in **information**. His merchant connections gave him a level of access that few others had—he could walk into British-controlled areas without raising suspicion, eavesdrop on officers in taverns, and move supplies under the guise of commerce. **If war was coming, the revolutionaries needed every advantage.**

By 1774, he had cemented himself as a trusted ally to the **Sons of Liberty**, though always careful to keep his profile low. He had attended meetings, listening but rarely speaking, ensuring that key moments stayed on course. **The Suffolk Resolves**, which called for open defiance of British rule, had passed in September of that year. He had been there, unseen in the background, as colonial leaders debated how far they were willing to go.

Then came the **Powder Alarm** in September. When British troops moved to seize gunpowder stores, the colonies responded with a **massive militia mobilization**—thousands of armed men gathered, convinced that war had begun. It was a false alarm, but the message was clear: **the people were ready.**

Calvin saw an opportunity.

As he sat in the **Green Dragon Tavern**, sipping a cup of coffee—his import business now flourishing thanks to the tea boycott—he leaned in as a group of men spoke in hushed voices. The British had spies, and the colonists needed their own network. They needed **intelligence**, a way to gather and move information without it being intercepted.

He set his cup down and spoke for the first time that evening. "Gentlemen, I may know a way."

The men looked at him, curiosity piqued. Samuel Adams, always skeptical, leaned back in his chair. "And what do you propose, Mercer?"

Calvin smiled. "A network of informants. A ring of trusted men and women who can pass messages **without suspicion**. The British use spies, but so can we. They move through the cities unnoticed. We should do the same."

John Hancock stroked his chin. "It would have to be **discreet**. Secrecy is key."

Calvin nodded. "We use symbols. Hidden messages. Codes that only we understand. It wouldn't be the first time smugglers used such tactics."

Sam grinned. "You seem well-versed in such things."

Calvin chuckled. "A merchant must know how to **protect his assets.**"

That night, the first discussions of **what would one day become the Culper Ring** began. Calvin knew it was too early for the full network to take shape—that would come years later—but the seeds were being planted.

As he left the tavern and stepped into the cold Boston night, he exhaled, watching his breath drift into the air. **The time for war was close.** And he had just helped give the revolutionaries one of their most valuable weapons.

# CHAPTER 28: THE MIDNIGHT MESSENGER

The flickering candlelight cast long shadows across the walls of the Green Dragon Tavern, where some of the most pivotal discussions of the revolution were taking place. Calvin sat quietly at a table with the Sons of Liberty, listening intently as Dr. Joseph Warren, Paul Revere, Samuel Adams, and John Hancock debated the inevitable confrontation looming over Massachusetts. The British were preparing to move. Everyone in the room knew it.

"The redcoats have their orders," Warren said, his voice low but firm. "General Gage has decided to seize our stores of gunpowder and weapons at Concord. They mean to break our will before war can even begin."

Revere leaned forward, his fingers drumming against the wooden table. "We must be ready. When they march, we ride."

Calvin studied Revere closely. The man was intelligent, resourceful, and unwavering in his dedication. **But history showed just how delicate this moment was.** Paul Revere's famous ride wasn't just about spreading the alarm; it was about ensuring that Lexington and Concord happened exactly as they were supposed to.

Calvin cleared his throat. "If the British move by land, you'll go across the Boston Neck. But if they move by water, you'll need another route." He turned to Warren. "You have someone ready to signal from the Old North Church?"

Warren nodded. "Two lanterns if they come by sea, one if by land."

Calvin exhaled, relieved that part was already in motion. But there was more to do. "Paul, you'll have to be careful. If the British catch you, the warning dies with you."

Revere smirked. "I have no intention of getting caught, friend."

Calvin knew better. *You will be caught,* he thought. *And you will be released. But others must make sure the warning reaches Concord.*

"What of Dawes?" Calvin asked, referring to **William Dawes**, who was to ride the southern route. "If Revere is delayed, we need another way to ensure the militia is ready."

"I'll ride out ahead," Dawes assured him. "They won't stop both of us."

Calvin nodded. But there was still one more thing. **The battle itself.** He had to ensure that when the British arrived in Lexington, the first shot was fired. It would not be a massacre, but it had to happen.

"The Lexington militia must be ready to stand their ground," Calvin said. "No one runs."

Samuel Adams crossed his arms. "Aye, but they must not fire first. Let the redcoats show the world who the aggressors are."

Calvin forced himself to remain calm. He knew how the battle began. He knew that hesitation might prevent the inevitable. **Would he need to intervene again?**

He looked at the men around the table. They were ready for war. The question was, would history cooperate?

As the meeting concluded, Calvin leaned toward Paul Revere. "Ride fast. Ride hard. And if you fall, someone else must carry the message."

Revere clapped him on the shoulder. "Don't worry, Mercer. We all have our roles to play."

Calvin forced a smile, but inside, he was already planning his next move. The fate of the revolution was about to be decided, and he was running out of time.

Calvin gripped the reins tightly as his horse thundered down the darkened road, the cool night air biting at his face. The **Old North Church** was behind him, and he couldn't help but feel a pang of regret. **It must have been incredible to see the lanterns placed in the bell tower, the signal that would set history in motion.** But he didn't have time to admire history unfolding— he had to be ahead of it.

Paul Revere would be right behind him soon, riding to warn the countryside. But Calvin needed to make sure that nothing prevented Revere from making it to Lexington. **There were too many variables, too many chances for failure.**

The trees closed in around the road as he rode through **Charlestown**, heading westward. The moon cast long shadows, making every movement in the underbrush seem like an ambush waiting to happen. He knew **British patrols** were out —Gage's spies were everywhere, and they would be looking for men like Revere and Dawes.

Calvin's heart pounded in his chest. He had prepared for this moment for years, but now that it was happening, it felt surreal. He was no longer an observer—**he was a participant in the single most important event of the Revolution's beginning.**

Ahead, he spotted a lantern swinging in slow arcs from a lone rider waiting near a crossroads. Calvin slowed his horse, pulling up beside **William Dawes**, who was waiting to confirm that Revere's ride was underway.

"You're ahead of him," Dawes noted, his voice low. "That part of the plan?"

Calvin nodded. "Making sure the road is clear."

Dawes gave him a knowing look but didn't press further. They both knew the stakes were too high for ego or hesitation. Dawes spurred his horse forward, heading toward his own route to spread the warning. Calvin, however, pressed ahead, ensuring the path toward **Lexington** was free of British patrols that might catch Revere before he could warn Adams and Hancock.

After nearly an hour of hard riding, Calvin pulled up at **Buckman Tavern**, the heart of Lexington's militia gathering. The town was quiet, the houses dark, but that wouldn't last. He slid from his saddle, rubbing his stiff hands together, and stepped inside.

Inside, a handful of men sat by the hearth, their voices hushed. **Captain John Parker**, leader of the Lexington militia, looked up at Calvin's entrance.

Calvin leaned against the wooden counter. "They're coming."

Parker's jaw tensed. "You're sure?"

Calvin nodded. "Paul Revere will be here soon. When he arrives, you'll have your confirmation."

The men in the room exchanged glances, some nervous, some steely-eyed. They knew this day would come—but knowing it and **facing it** were two different things.

Parker exhaled through his nose and nodded. "We'll be ready."

Calvin stepped back out into the cold night, looking eastward.

A flicker of movement down the road caught his attention. His stomach clenched. Something wasn't right. He strained his ears and caught the **distant sound of hoofbeats**, but they weren't coming from the direction of Boston—these were **British patrols moving in the dark**, setting up a blockade. If they intercepted Revere before he reached Lincoln, history could spiral off course.

Cursing under his breath, Calvin mounted his horse, kicking it into motion. He rode hard, cutting across a side path that would take him parallel to the main road. He needed to see exactly what the British were up to.

Ten minutes later, he pulled up behind a thick line of trees, peering through the branches. **A group of British regulars was stationed at a key crossroads leading into Lincoln.** They weren't moving—they were waiting.

A trap.

Calvin's pulse quickened. If they stopped Revere **before** Lincoln, there was no guarantee he would be released, and if the alarm failed to spread in time, Lexington might never happen.

His fingers tightened on the reins. He had two options: **trust fate, or intervene.**

Fate had brought him this far, but he wasn't about to gamble on it now.

For the first time since arriving in the past, he reached for his weapons, carefully secured in leather holsters strapped to the sides of his horse, hidden beneath a rolled tarp and a saddlebag to avoid drawing unwanted attention. Hidden in a false-bottomed section, he pulled out two muskets—at least, they appeared to be muskets. One was a **sniper rifle**, disguised to look like a long rifle, its sleek metal barrel coated in a hand-forged casing to make it indistinguishable from those of the era. The second was an **assault rifle**, meticulously modified to resemble a standard flintlock musket, complete with a false hammer and pan to deceive even the closest inspection. Both were designed to **sound and smoke like traditional muskets**, but they were anything but.

He checked the limited ammunition he had brought— **small-caliber rounds, carefully concealed in paper-wrapped cartridges, appearing no different than the common musket balls of the time. The muskets themselves were weighted and**

**balanced to match period weapons, ensuring they would not arouse suspicion even in the hands of a seasoned soldier.** He hoped he wouldn't need to fire a single shot. But if something went wrong tonight, if Revere was intercepted, if the British deviated from their course, he would have to ensure history **stayed on track.**

With a deep breath, Calvin slung both weapons across his back and returned his focus to the road ahead. The road stretched into darkness, but soon, a lone rider would emerge, carrying history on his back.

He swung off his horse and moved toward the treeline, keeping low. He unstrapped the **sniper rifle** and took a deep breath. He couldn't kill any of them—dead British soldiers would alter history—but he could certainly **make them hesitate.**

Lining up his shot, he aimed at a lantern hanging from one of the soldiers' saddles and squeezed the trigger.

CRACK!

The shot rang out, and the lantern exploded into a shower of glass and flame. The horses reared, men shouted in alarm, and chaos erupted among the patrol. Calvin fired another round, striking the wooden fencepost near their position, sending splinters flying.

"Snipers!" one of the officers shouted. "Take cover!"

Calvin smirked. No one in this era knew what a sniper was, but the **fear** in their voices told him it didn't matter. The British patrol scattered, diving behind their mounts or scrambling to find cover.

That was all he needed.

He slung the rifle back over his shoulder, leapt onto his horse, and galloped back toward the main road. He had just bought **Revere a clear path to Lincoln.**

As he rode, Calvin forced himself to breathe, pushing down the rush of adrenaline. He had just directly altered history, but only in a way that **restored** its course. No one had died. No name would change in the books.

And when Paul Revere rode past that very spot a short while later, he did so **unhindered.**

Calvin exhaled, watching from the shadows. **One crisis averted.**

Now, he had to make sure he reached Lexington in time for the next one.

Paul Revere was coming.

And behind him, the British army was marching.

# CHAPTER 29: THE SHOT THAT STARTS IT ALL

Calvin stood in the center of Lexington Green, shifting uneasily as the first streaks of dawn touched the horizon. The early morning air was cold and damp, carrying the scent of dew-soaked grass and distant wood smoke. Around him, nervous whispers and the shuffling of boots filled the silence as the Lexington militia—farmers, blacksmiths, and tradesmen—stood in uneasy ranks, muskets in hand.

Captain **John Parker**, his weathered face set with determination, moved among his men, offering quiet words of encouragement. But Calvin saw it in their eyes—**fear, uncertainty.** These men had drilled, but this wasn't practice anymore. **This was real.**

The British were coming.

Calvin knew that Revere had been **captured in Lincoln**, just as history had recorded. The warning had still spread, but Calvin's earlier skirmish had **unnerved the British patrols**. They were now **jumpy, wary, alert for unseen threats**. That might be enough to make them fire first.

But what if it wasn't?

Calvin's heart pounded as he scanned the tree line. He could hear them now—the rhythmic march of British **redcoats**, the metallic clink of **bayonets** shifting in formation. They were close.

He turned slightly and ran a hand along his musket—**the disguised sniper rifle** strapped securely to his side. He had ammunition, but he prayed he wouldn't have to use it. His entire mission came down to this moment. If the British did not fire first, the revolution **might not ignite as it should.**

A ripple of movement among the militia caught his eye—**some of the younger men shifted uneasily, gripping their muskets tighter**. One near Calvin, barely older than sixteen, licked his lips and muttered, "What if they don't stop?"

Calvin took a deep breath, steadying himself. "They will," he said softly. **"They always do."**

The first British soldiers appeared over the rise, their scarlet coats stark against the pale morning mist. **Hundreds of them.**

A British officer—**Major John Pitcairn**—rode forward, his voice sharp and commanding. "Lay down your arms! Disperse, you damned rebels!"

Captain Parker squared his jaw. "Stand your ground," he said to his men, his voice firm but quiet. "Don't fire unless fired upon. But if they mean to have a war, let it begin here."

A tense silence fell over the green, punctuated only by the stamping of horses and the rattle of musket barrels.

Calvin clenched his fists. **Was this it? Would one of the British fire? Or would history stall?**

A shout rang out from the British lines, and then—

*BANG!*

The first shot cracked through the dawn.

For a heartbeat, no one moved. The sound hung in the air, stretching impossibly long.

Then—

Chaos.

The British opened fire. A volley of musket balls tore through the still morning, striking wood, dirt, flesh. **Militiamen fell.** Others **fired back**, some out of fear, some out of rage.

Calvin ducked, his heart hammering. **History had happened.** The war had begun.

He exhaled a breath he hadn't realized he was holding. He had been ready to intervene, but **fate had taken its own course.**

Around him, the militia **broke apart**, retreating into the woods, firing sporadically as they fell back toward **Concord**. The British surged forward, pressing their advantage.

Calvin gritted his teeth. The **next phase** was beginning.

Lexington had been the spark.

Now, Concord would be the fire.

# CHAPTER 30: THE FIRE AT CONCORD

The British had pushed through Lexington, forcing the militia to scatter, but Calvin knew that the real test was still ahead. Concord.

The sun had fully risen by the time Calvin arrived, his horse lathered and breathing hard. He dismounted near **Colonel James Barrett's farm**, where militia leaders were hurriedly preparing their men. He could see the **North Bridge** in the distance, the British forces massing on one side while the growing ranks of colonial militia took positions on the other.

The tension in the air was thick, **charged with unspoken rage and anticipation.** The British had marched forward, burned supplies, and destroyed property—but now they were trapped between the bridge and the advancing militia.

Calvin moved among the men, nodding to those he recognized. He was no longer just an observer. **He was in this.**

Captain Isaac Davis of Acton's militia, a strong-willed leader, turned to Barrett. "We have no choice," he said, gripping his musket tight. "If they mean to take our homes, we must resist."

Barrett exhaled slowly and nodded. "We will march. But we will not fire first."

Calvin ground his teeth. **Always the same risk.** What if history wavered? What if the hesitation caused the moment to break?

The militia began advancing down the hill toward the bridge. Calvin fell in beside them, his disguised musket slung over his shoulder. He kept an eye on the British—**they were nervous, shifting their positions, their muskets unsteady in their hands.** His earlier actions outside Lincoln had rattled them.

The first British officer shouted, "Disperse, you rebels!"

No one moved.

The militia closed the distance, step by step.

One of the younger British soldiers twitched, lifting his musket slightly—

BANG!

A shot rang out, cracking through the crisp morning air. No one knew who fired first, but it didn't matter. The British **opened fire**, their muskets spewing smoke and lead.

The militia **returned fire.** The first British soldiers fell, and panic took hold of the redcoats. They had expected resistance, but not **this.**

"Hold the line!" a British officer bellowed, but his men were already **breaking.**

The militia surged forward, their blood boiling. Calvin took a position behind a tree, raised his rifle, and **fired—not to kill, but to push.** His shots struck the ground near the British soldiers, **forcing them to keep moving, to stay disoriented.**

The British tried to retreat in an orderly fashion, but their men were **panicked, confused, falling over themselves.**

By the time they reached the main road, it was no longer a retreat—it was **a rout.**

And the long road back to Boston had begun.

Calvin rode ahead along the side roads, keeping just far enough to watch but not be seen. The **entire countryside had erupted.**

Farmers, tradesmen, and militiamen poured out from their homes, taking up positions along the road. The British soldiers, exhausted and disorganized, **were being harassed the entire way back.**

Calvin took shots where he could, never aiming to hit, just enough to keep the British **moving, running, unable to regroup.**

By the time they reached **Charlestown**, the once-feared British army was **a broken force.**

Calvin exhaled, his hands shaking. He had been more than a witness today.

He had been a part of history.

And war had truly begun.

# CHAPTER 31: THE HEAT OF BUNKER HILL

The smoke from Concord had barely cleared when whispers of the British making another move began to circulate. The colonists were digging in, fortifying the high ground across the Charles River, and the British were preparing for an assault.

Calvin found himself **increasingly scrutinized.** He had tried to remain a shadow in the background, but it was impossible to ignore the murmurs in the streets—**who was this merchant who never seemed to be far from the flames of revolution?**

In the taverns, in meetings, in passing conversations, men were beginning to ask: **"Mercer, you always seem to know what's coming before it happens. How is that?"**

He had a ready answer. **"I trade in goods, but also in information. The British officers talk when they drink, and I listen."**

It was plausible. It explained why he had ears everywhere without ever openly taking up arms. But Calvin knew he was walking a fine line.

By mid-June, the British fleet in **Boston Harbor** had become a hive of activity. **Ships swarmed the waters, longboats ferrying soldiers to shore.**

Calvin met with **Joseph Warren and Israel Putnam**, two of the leaders in the effort to fortify Breed's Hill. He stood in the dirt among men stacking earthworks, sweat soaking their linen shirts despite the cool morning breeze.

"We hold this hill," Putnam said, his voice gravelly, "and we make them bleed for every inch."

Calvin kept his arms crossed, his expression unreadable. He had seen war before—**real war, modern war.** These men, as brave as they were, **had no idea what they were about to face.**

Warren clapped him on the shoulder. "You should take up a musket, Mercer. We could use another steady hand."

Calvin gave a tight smile. "I pass along information. That's all."

Warren smirked, eyes sharp. "Funny how you're always in the right place at the right time."

Calvin shrugged. "Call it a merchant's instinct."

Deep down, he knew he couldn't avoid this fight. **Bunker Hill was different. It was a turning point. A bloodbath that the British would 'win'—but at a cost that would shake them to their core.**

He needed to be there. He just had to decide **how involved he would be.**

# CHAPTER 32: THE BREAKING POINT

The roar of cannon fire shook the earth beneath Calvin's feet, the acrid scent of gunpowder thick in the June air. From his vantage point just behind the fortifications, he could see the British advancing in tight, disciplined ranks, their red coats a stark contrast against the dusty brown of the earthworks.

The militia around him were **nervous but resolute**, sweat streaming down their faces as they gripped their muskets tightly, waiting for the order to fire. Calvin knew how this battle would unfold—**twice the British would charge, and twice they would be repelled with devastating losses. But the third time...**

He gritted his teeth. He was supposed to be an observer, a shadow. He wasn't supposed to **change** anything, only to **ensure it happened as it should.** And yet, standing in the heart of the battle, that line was growing **blurred.**

He had both his **disguised muskets** strapped to his back, but he had no intention of using them. At least, that was the plan.

A shout echoed down the line. "Hold your fire... Hold...!"

The British came **closer, closer—**

"FIRE!"

The militia erupted in a crackling volley, sending British soldiers tumbling, their rigid formations breaking apart. The first wave faltered, then retreated down the hill. Cheers erupted around Calvin, men slapping each other on the back, emboldened. But Calvin's eyes were locked on the **second wave already forming.**

*They'll come again.*

And they did.

Another charge, another brutal exchange of fire. The redcoats fell by the dozens, their formations torn apart. Calvin could see the **uncertainty in their eyes**, the cracks forming in their discipline.

Then, the third charge.

**The breaking point.**

Calvin wiped sweat from his brow, his fingers tightening around the stock of his musket. Ammunition was running dangerously low. He could hear the **desperation in the shouted commands**, the frantic scrambling for powder and ball. **When the British charged again, the defenses would fail.**

Then, across the battlefield, Calvin saw **something that made his blood run cold.**

A British officer—a sharpshooter, musket braced against his shoulder—was lining up a shot.

Calvin's eyes followed the trajectory and landed on a man he **knew** was supposed to survive this battle. **Joseph Warren.**

His breath caught in his throat. *No.*

His mind raced. *This isn't supposed to happen. Warren is supposed to die—but not yet. Not like this.*

His body moved before his mind could argue. He dropped into a crouch, yanking the **sniper rifle** from his back and bracing it against the barricade. His heart pounded, his breaths coming shallow and rapid.

He had never killed anyone before. Even in all his careful interventions, he had always found a way to keep history intact **without spilling blood.**

But this wasn't about history anymore. **This was about Warren.**

He exhaled, steadied the barrel, and squeezed the trigger.

The disguised musket cracked like any other, smoke billowing from the barrel. Across the field, the British sharpshooter's body jerked violently, his musket falling from his grasp as he collapsed onto the grass.

Calvin lowered his rifle, his hands **shaking.** The moment stretched, the weight of what he had done pressing down on his chest.

He had **killed a man.**

But then, horror struck him. *Was that man supposed to live?* His mind reeled. *Would he have missed? Would Warren have survived anyway? Did I just destroy the history I was supposed to protect?*

He barely had time to process it before the British **broke through.** The militia was retreating. He had to move.

Slipping his rifle onto his back, Calvin fell in with the others, running down the hill, his heart hammering against his ribs.

The **Battle of Bunker Hill** was over.

And Calvin Mercer had just crossed a line he could never uncross.

# CHAPTER 33: THE WATCHFUL SHADOW

The war had pressed forward, and with each passing month, Calvin kept waiting for the moment when history would show its cracks. The moment where he would realize he had undone everything. But it never came.

Two years had passed since Bunker Hill, and yet, nothing had veered off course—at least, not in ways he could measure. **George Washington still commanded the Continental Army. The revolution still raged on.** If Calvin had broken something, it wasn't obvious.

But that didn't mean it wouldn't be.

Calvin had spent those years **watching, listening, waiting**—and ensuring he remained nothing more than a whisper in the background of history. His business had flourished. He had become a trader of goods and, more importantly, a **trader of information.**

His **spy network had expanded**, not in the dramatic fashion of a revolutionary mastermind, but in **small, deliberate steps**. Couriers, tavern owners, dockworkers—men and women who picked up rumors and passed them along without even realizing they were doing it. Calvin's money, earned through legitimate trade, kept the wheels of this network greased. He paid for information, **bribed the right people, silenced the wrong ones.**

And through it all, he made sure one thing was clear—**Calvin Mercer was no hero.**

There were times when history brushed past him—**he stood in the crowd as Thomas Paine's *Common Sense* swept the colonies in early 1776. He heard whispers of the push for independence before the Declaration was even drafted.** He was always **there**, just on the edge, but never at the center.

One night, as he sat in a dimly lit tavern in Philadelphia, a familiar voice cut through the low murmur of conversation.

"You know, Mercer, for a man who insists he's just a merchant, you always seem to be exactly where the storm is brewing."

Calvin turned slowly, offering a thin smile. The man across from him was **Benjamin Tallmadge**, a young but sharp officer in Washington's service.

"I hear a great many things," Calvin said smoothly, sipping from his cup. "That doesn't mean I make them happen."

Tallmadge leaned forward, his eyes sharp. "Perhaps. But men like you don't just observe, Mercer. They choose their moments."

Calvin tilted his head. "And what is it you think I've chosen?"

Tallmadge smirked. "That's what I'm trying to figure out."

He leaned in, lowering his voice. "You've got ears everywhere, Mercer. A network—small, but effective. I'd wager you know more about British troop movements than half the officers in Washington's camp."

Calvin sipped his drink, weighing his response. "I'm a businessman. I keep informed."

Tallmadge chuckled, but his eyes stayed locked on Calvin. "A businessman who trades in whispers more than goods? It's not just curiosity, Mercer. Washington needs good intelligence. We're assembling something—something bigger than loose rumors and gut feelings. And I think you could be a valuable asset."

Calvin felt the weight of the moment pressing down on him. **The Culper Ring wasn't supposed to exist yet.** Not officially. **Was this the moment that set it in motion?**

He exhaled slowly. "Let's say I do have a network. Let's say I pass along information when it serves the right people. The moment I step into something official, I become part of history. And that's not something I want."

Tallmadge studied him, tapping a finger against the rim of his mug. "You can't hide forever, Mercer. The war isn't won in the field alone. It's won in the shadows, in the messages that never see the light of day. You could help in ways no one else could."

Calvin hesitated. **Should he tell him? Should he hand over what he had built, push history in the right direction?**

Or would that alter something he couldn't undo?

He forced a smirk. "I'll think about it."

Tallmadge didn't look convinced. "You do that. But don't take too long, Mercer. The war waits for no man."

The words sat heavy between them, but Calvin held his silence. He had spent two years ensuring no one would remember him as a founding father or a revolutionary hero.

And yet, men like Tallmadge—**men who built spy networks, who played the long game**—were starting to notice him. That wasn't good.

He needed to be careful.

As the war pressed toward **Valley Forge**, Calvin knew his role wasn't done. **He still had history to protect.** But how much longer could he stay in the shadows before someone pulled him into the light?

# CHAPTER 34: THE FORGE OF WINTER

The barren landscape of Valley Forge stretched before Calvin as he rode through the camp, his breath visible in the frigid air. The ground was frozen solid, the skeletal remains of trees reaching skyward like desperate hands. Smoke curled from makeshift huts, where soldiers huddled together, their ragged clothes doing little to shield them from the brutal Pennsylvania winter.

Calvin pulled his cloak tighter around himself. He had seen warzones before, but nothing like this. **This wasn't just war. This was survival.**

Tallmadge rode beside him, guiding him toward the center of camp. "You wanted to see for yourself," Tallmadge said, his tone grim. "Here it is."

"I believed the reports," Calvin said, scanning the suffering around him. "I just needed to see it with my own eyes."

Tallmadge slowed his horse as they approached a large **canvas tent** near the heart of the camp. "General Washington wants to meet you."

Calvin tensed. He had been in the presence of many key figures in this war, but this was different. **George Washington wasn't just a name in history books—he was history itself.**

As they dismounted, an officer pulled back the tent flap, and Tallmadge gestured for Calvin to step inside. The warmth from a small fire **did little to cut through the tension.**

Washington sat at a table strewn with **maps and reports**, his piercing eyes lifting as Calvin entered. He was taller than Calvin had expected, his presence filling the space in a way that made the tent seem smaller.

"So," Washington said, his voice calm but carrying the weight of command, "you are the elusive Mr. Mercer."

Calvin inclined his head. "General."

Washington gestured to a chair. "Sit."

Calvin did, aware that Washington was studying him carefully. "You seem to have a knack for appearing where things are most uncertain."

Calvin gave a careful smile. "I have an interest in the success of this revolution, same as you."

Washington leaned forward. "Perhaps. But I know more about you than you might think."

Calvin tensed but kept his expression neutral. "Is that so?"

The general nodded. "Your name appears in many reports. Always on the edge of great events, yet never fully part of them. Men like Tallmadge trust you. Men like Adams listen when you speak. And yet, there is no record of where you came from before all of this."

Calvin exhaled slowly. **Washington was not a man easily deceived.**

"You've done your homework," Calvin said, keeping his tone even.

"I have," Washington replied. "And I find myself wondering—are you an asset to this cause or a danger to it?"

Calvin smirked. "I could ask the same of you, General."

Silence stretched between them. Then, to Calvin's surprise, **Washington smiled.**

"You know more than you should," Washington said finally. "You carry yourself like a man who knows how this all plays out."

Calvin's pulse quickened. *How much does he suspect?*

Washington leaned back. "I've also heard that you were in Boston before the massacre, that you had dealings with men like Adams and Revere long before most did. You had business in Concord, and somehow you always seem to be a step ahead of the British. That is a peculiar trait, Mr. Mercer."

Calvin forced himself to keep a straight face. "You do keep a thorough account, General."

Washington nodded. "It is my responsibility to know those within my camp. But I must admit, you remain an enigma. Where does a simple merchant acquire such foresight?"

Calvin leaned forward slightly. "Perhaps the same way you knew to cross the Delaware on Christmas night, knowing the Hessians would be too drunk to respond in time. Or how you had the instinct to fall back at Fort Necessity when you were a young officer, before most men your age would know what retreat even meant."

Washington's brow furrowed, and for the first time, his composed exterior cracked—just slightly. "Those are not matters commonly discussed."

Calvin allowed himself a small smile. "Neither are mine."

The tent fell into silence, the only sound the crackling of the fire. Washington studied him, his eyes narrowing slightly as if piecing together a puzzle he didn't yet understand. Finally, he gave a slow nod. "You know much for a man who does not seek power."

"And you are a man who inspires power without seeking it,"

Calvin replied smoothly.

Washington exhaled through his nose, a trace of amusement flashing in his eyes before his face settled back into its typical unreadable mask. "You've seen the suffering here. You know what's at stake. If you are truly committed to this cause, then prove it."

Calvin met his gaze. "What do you need?"

Washington didn't hesitate. "Supplies. Food. Medicine. We need whatever you can get, however you can get it."

Calvin nodded. "I'll see what I can do."

Washington studied him a moment longer, then nodded. "Then, Mr. Mercer, welcome to Valley Forge."

# CHAPTER 35: THE WEIGHT OF DECISIONS

The bitter cold of Valley Forge gnawed at Calvin as he sat alone in his quarters, staring at the single candle flickering atop his desk. Outside, the wind howled through the skeletal trees, carrying the distant groans of starving men. It wasn't just hunger—it was sickness, frostbite, despair. Washington's army was being tested in ways that history recorded as both their greatest struggle and their defining moment.

And Calvin could change it.

He had the means to send Washington all the food, medicine, and warm clothing he needed. If he pulled the right strings, the army could be resupplied within weeks. **No starvation, no amputated limbs lost to the cold, no men freezing to death in the night.**

But that wasn't what history recorded.

He slammed his fist against the desk in frustration. **Damn this war. Damn this mission.** He hated the thought of standing by while men suffered, but he had spent his entire time in the past ensuring that history flowed as it should. If he sent too much aid, he risked unraveling the very hardship that forged the army's resilience, the struggle that made the men revere Washington with an almost religious fervor.

But if he did nothing...

He ran a hand over his face, exhaustion weighing on him. There was a middle ground. **Small shipments. Enough to save lives, but not enough to rewrite history.**

The next morning, he met with Tallmadge outside the supply tents, where soldiers were rationing meager portions of spoiled bread and thin stew. The air was thick with the stench of unwashed bodies and disease, and Calvin felt his resolve nearly break.

"You've made your decision," Tallmadge said, his voice tight with controlled frustration.

Calvin nodded. "Small shipments. Quiet and untraceable."

Tallmadge exhaled sharply, shaking his head. "You could do more."

Calvin's jaw tightened. "And I could change everything."

Tallmadge studied him for a long moment, searching his face. Finally, he sighed and muttered, "Then let's pray it's enough."

That evening, a summons arrived. **Washington wanted to see him.**

Calvin entered the command tent with careful steps, his breath catching in the heavy silence. Washington stood at his desk, his fingers resting lightly on a stack of reports. The general didn't look up right away, and Calvin wasn't sure if the pause was intentional or simply the exhaustion of a man carrying the weight of a nation.

Finally, Washington lifted his gaze. "I understand you've arranged for supplies."

Calvin gave a small nod. "A few shipments. Quietly arranged."

Washington's blue eyes bore into him, unreadable. "Why so little?"

Calvin clenched his fists at his sides. "Because men must suffer to understand what they're fighting for. And because if I move too much, it brings attention to me, to my operations. I can currently move in and out of British-held territory unnoticed, I can gather information, I can ensure the right people hear the right things. If I suddenly become a lifeline of supplies, that all changes. The British would investigate, my contacts would dry up, and everything I've built would crumble."

A heavy silence settled between them.

Washington's voice was steady when he finally spoke. "That is a callous philosophy."

Calvin swallowed hard. "Perhaps. But necessary."

Washington's expression shifted—**not anger, not disappointment, but something close to recognition.** He had led men to battle. He had ordered attacks that cost lives for the greater good. He knew the weight of sacrifice.

"You are a difficult man to understand, Mr. Mercer," Washington admitted, his voice quieter now. "But I believe you are not without purpose."

Calvin exhaled. "I have no desire to see your army fail. But I also cannot be the man who changes what must happen."

Washington studied him carefully, absorbing the weight of those words. "You've sacrificed much for a man who claims to remain in the shadows. I wonder, Mr. Mercer, do you believe in this cause, or do you believe only in the preservation of what you think must happen?"

Calvin hesitated, then replied, "I believe in both. And sometimes, those two beliefs are at odds."

Washington nodded slowly, as if seeing something in Calvin that even he didn't fully grasp. "Then I will take what you offer and ask no more."

The tension in Calvin's chest loosened, but only slightly. **Would it be enough? Would history stay its course?**

As he stepped out into the night, he shivered—not from the cold, but from the lingering dread that he had already set changes in motion that he couldn't take back.

# CHAPTER 36: THE SEEDS OF THE CULPER RING

The winter stretched on, relentless in its cruelty. The soldiers at Valley Forge endured starvation, sickness, and frostbite, and despite his own reservations, Calvin continued his quiet shipments of supplies. Never enough to save the army outright, but just enough to keep them from collapsing entirely.

Through it all, Tallmadge remained by his side, a constant presence in this frozen hell. The two had formed a quiet understanding—**Calvin didn't explain his knowledge, and Tallmadge didn't pry.** But that didn't mean questions weren't brewing beneath the surface.

One evening, as they sat by a low-burning fire in the officer's quarters, Tallmadge leaned in. "I have a plan," he said, voice barely above a whisper.

Calvin raised an eyebrow. "You always have a plan."

Tallmadge smirked. "This one's different. The British have spies everywhere. They know too much, too quickly. Washington needs an intelligence network of his own."

Calvin exhaled, staring into the fire. **He knew what was coming. This was the beginning of the Culper Ring.**

"You want informants," Calvin said finally.

"I want an entire system," Tallmadge corrected. "A way to move messages that even the best British spies can't intercept. A network built on secrecy, on deception. Washington has given me permission to begin, but I need people I can trust."

Calvin met his gaze, his mind racing. **He could help.** His existing spy network, his connections—he could give Tallmadge exactly what he needed to lay the foundation.

But should he?

He turned the thought over in his mind. **If he held back, the Culper Ring would still form. But would it be weaker? Would it take longer? Would history falter?**

"You're hesitating," Tallmadge noted, watching him carefully. "Why?"

Calvin forced a smirk. "I don't like being noticed, Tallmadge."

Tallmadge chuckled. "Neither do spies."

A long silence stretched between them before Calvin finally nodded. "I can help."

Tallmadge grinned. "I had a feeling you would."

He leaned forward, eyes gleaming with intensity. "We can't rely on couriers alone. They're too easily intercepted. The British have too many eyes on the roads, and too many ears in the taverns. We need something better—something that doesn't look like a spy network."

Calvin nodded, rubbing his chin. "A merchant's ledger could be a good cover for coded messages. Transactions that don't exist. A system of false trades to move intelligence."

Tallmadge's eyebrows lifted. "You think like a spymaster already."

Calvin smirked. "I think like a man who prefers to keep his head attached to his shoulders."

Tallmadge chuckled. "Washington wants something reliable. A network based in New York, since that's where the British are strongest. We'll need cutouts—intermediaries who don't know the full chain of communication. The messages need to move without one person knowing the entire system."

Calvin frowned. "That means we need a reliable dead-drop system. Something that won't look suspicious."

Tallmadge nodded eagerly. "Exactly. A method where messages are passed through regular citizens, unaware of what they're carrying."

Calvin leaned back. "Laundry."

Tallmadge blinked. "Laundry?"

"Women in occupied towns hang their laundry out every day. A black petticoat on the line could mean 'urgent message.' A certain handkerchief could mean 'rendezvous at the tavern.' They'd never suspect a housewife of espionage."

Tallmadge tapped his fingers on his knee. "I like it. And invisible ink?"

Calvin hesitated. **He knew it would be developed, but had it been yet?** "Lemon juice," he said finally. "Write a message, heat the paper over a candle, and the words appear."

Tallmadge grinned. "That might just work."

Calvin smiled back. "It does work. I used to send messages this way to a girl." He said, his eyes shining.

Tallmadge laughed out loud.

Calvin let out a breath, staring into the fire. **This was happening. He was part of it now.** He had to ensure it played out correctly.

Tallmadge slapped him on the shoulder. "You, Mercer, are going to be very useful."

Calvin smirked but felt a chill creep into his gut. **Had he just taken another step toward rewriting history?**

As the fire crackled between them, Calvin stared into the flames, wondering if he had just made another change to history—one that he would never be able to take back.

# CHAPTER 37: A WAITING GAME

The days at Valley Forge stretched into weeks, then months. The snow had begun to melt, but the hardships remained. Calvin had done what he could without rewriting history—small shipments, strategic intelligence, whispers in the right ears. The suffering of the Continental Army continued, as it must. And yet, through it all, one thought persisted in his mind.
**Benedict Arnold.**

His final task.

He wasn't sure exactly when it would happen, but it loomed over him like a storm on the horizon. **When Arnold's betrayal came, Calvin had to ensure it unfolded the way history recorded.** Once that was done…maybe he could go home.

But first, there was the Culper Ring.

---

Calvin and Tallmadge sat in the officer's quarters late into the night, **the flickering candlelight casting shadows along the walls.** Maps, notes, and coded messages were strewn across the rough wooden table. **Tallmadge was methodical, a brilliant strategist, but even he was still learning the art of espionage.**

"This is bigger than just a few couriers," Tallmadge muttered, tapping his finger against the tabletop. "We need informants in the highest places—merchants, officers, even loyalists who are only loyal because they have to be."

Calvin leaned back in his chair, folding his arms. "That means money. A lot of it. These people aren't going to risk their necks for patriotism alone."

Tallmadge smirked. "Which is where you come in."

Calvin exhaled through his nose. "I figured as much."

"You've already got connections," Tallmadge continued. "Your network, your business—if we funnel some of that into financing our informants, we can keep this quiet and effective."

Calvin rubbed his temples. **He knew this would happen. He had been instrumental in setting up the foundation of this network, but now it was evolving.** He had to make sure it stayed on course.

"So, who do we trust?" Calvin asked finally.

Tallmadge straightened. "Abraham Woodhull. He's a farmer in Setauket, but he has the right temperament. His ties to the British make him seem harmless. He's reluctant, but I think I can convince him."

Calvin nodded. "Who else?"

"Anna Strong," Tallmadge replied. "She's clever, observant, and well-connected. She'll help with the signals—the laundry system you suggested."

Calvin smirked. "Glad to see you took that idea seriously."

Tallmadge chuckled. "It's simple and it works. That's what we need—systems that don't rely on chance."

Calvin drummed his fingers against the table. "And the actual messages?"

Tallmadge's expression darkened. "We need a way to move them that can't be traced. Couriers alone won't cut it. The British will be watching every movement. We need dead drops, coded letters, something that will pass unnoticed."

Calvin exhaled. "We need a cipher."

Tallmadge's eyes lit up. "Yes. A code only we can read. Something layered. I've been experimenting with a numbering system—assigning numbers to names, locations, phrases. It's crude, but it could work."

Calvin nodded slowly. "That's good. But what about counterintelligence? What happens when the British catch wind of this?"

Tallmadge hesitated. "Then we make sure they're always chasing ghosts."

Calvin let out a low chuckle. "I like the way you think."

---

The following weeks were a blur of meetings, planning, and careful execution. **The network began to take shape.** Messages moved through invisible hands, coded signals passed in plain sight, and information flowed like an underground river. Calvin stayed involved, but always on the periphery. **He had to make sure history stayed intact, but he also had to ensure that when the time came, he could walk away.**

One evening, as he sat in a dimly lit tavern in Philadelphia, Tallmadge slid into the seat across from him. He looked tired, but there was a gleam of satisfaction in his eyes.

"The ring is in place," Tallmadge said quietly. "It's working."

Calvin nodded. "Then my work here is almost done."

Tallmadge studied him. "You always talk like you're leaving."

Calvin forced a smirk. "Because one day, I will."

Tallmadge exhaled. "Well, you've done more than enough. If I didn't know better, I'd say you were sent here just to make sure this all happened."

Calvin's smirk faltered for just a second. "Maybe I was."

Tallmadge chuckled, shaking his head. "You're a mystery, Mercer. But I'm glad you're on our side."

Calvin lifted his mug. "To history."

Tallmadge raised his own. "To history."

As they drank, Calvin felt the weight of what was coming settle over him. **Benedict Arnold. The final test.**

And after that… home.

# CHAPTER 38: THE TRAITOR'S PATH

The Culper Ring was running like a well-oiled machine. The invisible threads of intelligence wove through occupied territory, carried by merchants, housewives, and unsuspecting couriers who never knew the weight of the information they ferried. The British were always one step behind, chasing whispers that faded before they could grasp them. Calvin had done what he set out to do. The ring belonged to Tallmadge now.

And now, **all of his focus was on Benedict Arnold.**

The irony wasn't lost on Calvin. If Arnold had died of his wounds at **Saratoga**, he would have gone down as a legend, a martyr for the cause, his name spoken with reverence alongside Washington and Greene. Instead, he would become **the greatest traitor in American history.**

It had taken years, but the pieces were falling into place. **Arnold had just been given command of West Point.** That meant **history was approaching a critical moment.**

Calvin sat in a quiet corner of a tavern in New York, nursing a drink as he ran through the facts in his head. **This was it.** His last mission. If he could make sure Arnold's betrayal happened as recorded, then history would remain intact, and—maybe, just maybe—he could finally go home.

The door swung open, and Tallmadge stepped inside, shaking off the autumn chill. His eyes scanned the room before landing on Calvin. He walked over, sliding into the seat across from him.

"You've been quiet," Tallmadge noted.

Calvin smirked. "That's rich, coming from you."

Tallmadge gave a dry chuckle but leaned in, his tone lowering. "Arnold has West Point. The British will make their move soon."

Calvin exhaled. "And we need to make sure he follows through."

Tallmadge frowned. "It still doesn't sit right with me. We could stop him now. We have enough to expose him."

Calvin clenched his jaw. "And if we do, what then? He's a war hero. Half of Congress adores him. If we accuse him now, we look paranoid at best, desperate at worst. And then what? Do we risk losing Washington's trust? Do we fracture the army?"

Tallmadge sighed. "You always think further ahead than the rest of us."

Calvin took a slow sip of his drink. *Further ahead than you'll ever know.*

The tavern door opened again. A courier entered, weaving through the tables before stopping beside Tallmadge and slipping him a folded note. Tallmadge read it quickly, his face tightening.

"It's happening," he murmured. "Arnold has made contact with the British. Major André is in play."

Calvin set his drink down, his fingers tightening around the tankard. **This was it.** The moment had arrived. If he played his part right, **history would stay its course.**

Tallmadge's eyes flicked up to Calvin's. "What now?"

Calvin exhaled, his mind racing. **He had to ensure that Arnold's betrayal was revealed at the right moment. Not too soon. Not**

**too late.**

He met Tallmadge's gaze. "Now? Now we let Arnold dig his own grave."

Tallmadge studied him for a long moment before nodding. "Then let's make sure the world remembers him for what he truly is."

Calvin forced a smile. **Oh, they would.**

And after this... he might finally be free.

# CHAPTER 39: THE CAPTURE OF BENEDICT ARNOLD

The autumn air was crisp as Calvin stood on the high ridges overlooking the Hudson River. The golden hues of the changing leaves were deceptive—this was a battlefield in waiting. West Point sat at the heart of America's defensive line, and Arnold had just made the first move to sell it to the British.

He gritted his teeth. **All it would take was one slip, and everything could unravel.**

Tallmadge rode up beside him, dismounting quickly. "We intercepted André," he said, breathless from the ride. "He was disguised as a civilian and carrying the plans to West Point."

Calvin exhaled sharply. "And Arnold?"

"He's still in West Point, but once word reaches him, he'll flee."

Calvin nodded. He already knew how this played out—**Arnold would escape, running straight into British hands, while André would be captured and executed.** Still, he had to make sure it went that way.

The two men rode toward the fort, where **Washington himself**

**had just arrived, oblivious to the treachery underfoot.** Inside, Arnold sat in his quarters, poring over maps. His posture was rigid, as if he knew something was wrong but hadn't confirmed it yet.

A knock at the door startled him. Calvin and Tallmadge entered, keeping their expressions neutral.

"Gentlemen," Arnold greeted stiffly. "To what do I owe the pleasure?"

Tallmadge stepped forward. "Major André was caught."

Arnold paled. His fingers twitched, and for the briefest moment, Calvin saw something flicker across his face—**panic.**

"I see," Arnold said slowly. "What... what was he doing?"

Calvin decided to push. "Carrying plans. To West Point."

Arnold's jaw tightened. "Then I assume he is in custody?"

"For now," Tallmadge confirmed. "But we expect Washington will order his execution."

Arnold stood quickly, his chair scraping against the wooden floor. "If you'll excuse me, I have business to attend to."

Calvin watched as Arnold collected a few belongings, stuffing them into his coat with forced calm. **This was it. The moment where Arnold made his escape.**

"You're leaving?" Calvin asked, feigning curiosity.

Arnold forced a laugh. "Of course not. Just handling affairs."

Calvin nodded. "Safe travels."

Arnold hesitated for a fraction of a second. Then, **without another word, he left.**

Tallmadge turned to Calvin. "We could stop him."

Calvin shook his head. "No. He has to run. Let him go."

Tallmadge clenched his jaw but nodded. **They had their traitor.**

Hours later, Washington returned to the fort, and when he heard of Arnold's flight, **his fury was volcanic.** But despite his anger, the betrayal worked to his advantage—**Arnold's treason rallied the American cause, uniting the army against a new villain.**

As Calvin watched the events unfold, he exhaled in relief. **History was intact.**

Now, all that remained was for him to find a way home.

# CHAPTER 40: TYING UP LOOSE ENDS

The long ride back to Massachusetts was both a relief and a weight on Calvin's mind. He had done everything he was meant to do—every piece of history had unfolded as expected. The Revolution would survive. The nation would be born. But now, in the wake of it all, Calvin felt an unfamiliar sensation creeping into his bones.
What now?

The question gnawed at him as he rode through the rolling countryside, the air crisp with the scent of autumn leaves. **This was home, yet it wasn't.** Not really. He had lived in this time for years, but it still wasn't his. **His mission was complete. That meant it was time to leave… right?**

He pushed those thoughts aside as he approached his estate. His home—built through careful deception, legitimate trade, and a network of relationships—stood unchanged, a quiet refuge on the outskirts of Boston. It was **a merchant's house, a spy's hideaway, a historian's tomb.**

Inside, he went through his ledgers, clearing debts, finalizing shipments, ensuring that everything was in order. He **paid off the last of his couriers**, the men and women who had unknowingly moved intelligence across the colonies. He sent final instructions to his business associates, ensuring that his absence wouldn't be questioned.

By the time he was done, the sun had dipped below the horizon, casting long shadows across his study. He poured himself a drink, the burn of the liquor doing little to calm his nerves. **There was one last thing to do.**

Calvin had spent years buried in war and espionage, but now, with time to spare, he did what he had always wanted to do since arriving—**he explored.**

For the first time since arriving in the past, he **allowed himself to be a tourist.** He walked the cobbled streets of Boston, tracing the steps of the Revolution not as a participant but as an observer. **He stood at the site of the Boston Massacre, feeling the weight of history pressing down on him.**

He visited Paul Revere's home, suppressing a smirk as he overheard people discussing Revere's legendary ride—**knowing full well how much effort it had taken to ensure it happened at all.**

At the harbor, he stood on the very docks where the Boston Tea Party had begun, watching the ships rock gently in the water. The past was alive around him, **but he no longer belonged to it.**

One evening, as he sat alone in the Green Dragon Tavern, an old acquaintance—a former Sons of Liberty member—clapped him on the shoulder. "Mercer, you've been a ghost lately. Thinking of leaving us?"

Calvin gave a small smile. "Something like that."

The man laughed. "Where would you go? The war's still raging, you know."

Calvin swirled his drink, staring into the amber liquid. "Somewhere far away."

The man chuckled again, shaking his head. "Well, if you do, don't be a stranger. You always seem to know what's going to happen before it does."

Calvin forced a smirk. *You have no idea.*

As the tavern buzzed with conversation around him, he **felt the weight of finality settling in.** He had done what he came to do. The pages of history had been written as they were always meant to be.

Now, he just had to find his way back to the present.

# CHAPTER 41: THE SIGNAL

The morning air was crisp as Calvin stood in the middle of the field, the same spot where he had arrived years ago. The sky stretched overhead, pale blue with wisps of clouds, and for the first time in a long time, he was alone—truly alone.

He reached into his coat pocket and pulled out the **pocket watch** —an intricate piece of metal and glass, far too advanced for this time. It had never been a simple timepiece. It was **his way home.**

He ran his fingers over the smooth, familiar surface, taking in the weight of it. He had thought about this moment for so long, envisioned it, anticipated it, dreaded it. **Would it really work? Or had he changed too much?**

He inhaled deeply and flipped it open.

The dials on the watch shimmered, the faint glow of circuitry coming to life beneath the glass. He pressed the hidden sequence he had memorized before ever stepping into the past.

The watch's face lit up **green.**

For a moment, nothing happened.

Then a low **hum** filled the air, the static-like crackle of energy pulsing around him. The air thickened, charged with something unseen. A split second later, there was a flash of **light.** Then it was gone.

Calvin exhaled, waiting. **Nothing.**

Another flash. A crackling sound. **Then silence.**

A third time. **Still nothing.**

He frowned, gripping the watch tightly. **Something was wrong.**

Then, **out of nowhere, a small object appeared in front of him** —a scrap of paper, weighted down by a rock. Calvin's stomach dropped as he bent to pick it up, immediately recognizing the messy handwriting.

**Park's handwriting.**

With a deep breath, he unfolded the note.

Three words. Simple. Devastating.

**"It's not working."**

The world seemed to tilt. He stared at the words, willing them to change, to say something else, to give him an answer.

His heart pounded in his chest. **What now?**

The field was silent, the wind rustling through the grass as if whispering an answer he couldn't hear.

Calvin closed his eyes, swallowing down the rising panic. **He was stuck.**

And for the first time since arriving in this time, **he had no idea what came next.**

# CHAPTER 42: A LEGACY SET IN STONE

The years passed like a slow-moving tide, wearing away at the urgency Calvin once felt. There was no way home—at least, not yet. His life as a merchant continued, his fortune growing as he maneuvered through post-war America. He still kept his distance from anything that could alter history, watching from the shadows as the country took its first unsteady steps toward nationhood.

The Revolution had ended. **The United States was real.** And though he had played a role, **his name would never be written in the history books.**

Calvin kept his head down, kept working, and waited. **Always waiting.**

---

The streets of Washington, D.C. bustled with activity, the air thick with anticipation. The city had become the center of the new government, and excitement buzzed like static in the air. Calvin moved through the newly established capital, listening to the murmurs of a nation being built. **The Constitution had been ratified. Washington had been elected.** The future was taking shape before his eyes, just as history had dictated it would.

He stood near the edge of the construction site, where workers moved stone and timber, laying the foundation for what they called the **"President's Mansion" in the new capital of Washington, D.C.** A grand building, a symbol of leadership, though **its true significance wouldn't be recognized for years.**

Calvin exhaled slowly. **This was it.**

He had one more task to complete.

---

Under the cover of night, Calvin moved through the unfinished structure, the bones of the mansion standing stark against the moonlit sky. **He had prepared for this moment for years.** The safe—**his final message to the future**—was crafted with care, designed with mechanisms that would **only allow one person to open it at a precise moment in time.**

No one in this century could ever access it.

With careful precision, he embedded it into the foundation, in a secluded corner of the mansion where it would be unnoticed, forgotten—until it was needed.

He ran his fingers over the cool metal of the safe, securing it in place. Inside was **the truth.** His letter. His warning. **The reason why history had to happen exactly as it did.**

He stepped back, exhaling as he surveyed his work. **Would they ever find it?**

Would they ever send him home?

For now, there was nothing more he could do.

He turned away, disappearing into the night as the mansion rose above him, brick by brick, into what the world would one day know as **the White House.**

# EPILOGUE

The Oval Office was quiet. The day had been long, filled with meetings, briefings, and the never-ending weight of the world pressing down on the President's shoulders. With a sigh, he closed the last folder on his desk and stood, stretching as he prepared to leave for the night.

Just as he turned to go, **the door opened.**

He frowned. It wasn't his security detail or his personal staff. Instead, a small group of White House personnel entered, the kind of people who had been there long before his administration and would remain long after he was gone. **Archivists, preservationists, and custodians of the building's deepest secrets.**

The President looked at them warily. **He recognized them, of course, but these were not his chosen people.** They were part of something bigger—something older.

"What's this about?" he asked, his tone cautious.

One of the senior staff members stepped forward. "Mr. President, there is a secret that only a select few have been entrusted with. For over two centuries, we and those who came before us have kept it." He gestured toward the others. "Tonight, it is time to pass that secret on to you."

The President hesitated. "A secret?"

"We ask that you come with us."

He glanced between their solemn faces, waiting for an explanation, but none came. The air in the room felt heavier, **as if the walls themselves were holding their breath.** Finally, he nodded. "Lead the way."

They took him deep into the White House, past hallways he rarely walked, into a section of the building that felt **almost untouched by time.** Finally, they stopped in a dimly lit corner, where one of the staff members reached for the wall and, with a subtle press, moved **a hidden panel.**

Behind it sat **an old, weathered safe.**

The President stared at it, his brow furrowing. "What is this?"

The senior staff member shook his head. "We don't know. None of us do. We only have instructions—passed down through generations—to bring the sitting President here on this date, at this time."

The President stepped closer, running his hand over the metal. It was ancient, worn by time, yet still unyielding. The combination lock was there, unbroken, untouched.

"I don't know the combination," he admitted.

The staff merely watched him, expectant. **Silent.**

With a deep breath, he reached for the handle and gave it a turn.

**The safe opened.**

Gasps filled the room. The staff who had spent their careers preserving the secrets of the White House stood in awe. Some exchanged glances, others merely stared. **The safe had never been opened before.**

Inside, resting atop a velvet cloth, was **a leather-bound notebook, aged and delicate but perfectly preserved.** It was tied with string, as though it had been placed there only yesterday.

The President carefully lifted it out, untied the string, and opened to the first page.

The handwriting was **crisp, deliberate.**

**Dear Mr. President,**

**My name is Calvin Mercer, and this is my story...**

Made in the USA
Monee, IL
14 March 2025

14013584R00089